SPECIAL MESS

THE ULVERSCH
(registered UK cl

was established in 1972 to provide funds for research, diagnosis and treatment of eye diseases. Examples of major projects funded by the Ulverscroft Foundation are:-

- The Children's Eye Unit at Moorfields Eye Hospital, London
- The Ulverscroft Children's Eye Unit at Great Ormond Street Hospital for Sick Children
- Funding research into eye diseases and treatment at the Department of Ophthalmology, University of Leicester
- The Ulverscroft Vision Research Group, Institute of Child Health
- Twin operating theatres at the Western Ophthalmic Hospital, London
- The Chair of Ophthalmology at the Royal Australian College of Ophthalmologists

You can help further the work of the Foundation by making a donation or leaving a legacy. Every contribution is gratefully received. If you would like to help support the Foundation or require further information, please contact:

THE ULVERSCROFT FOUNDATION
The Green, Bradgate Road, Anstey
Leicester LE7 7FU, England
Tel: (0116) 236 4325

website: www.foundation.ulverscroft.com

Matthew Malekos is an ex-psychiatric nurse. He lives on the island of Cyprus with his civil partner.

SNOW WASTED

Forensic pathologist Dr Karen Laos is approached by the Ministry of Defence and dispatched as a civilian contractor to Cyprus. A soldier stationed on the island has been murdered, the crime bearing similarities to the killing of another serviceman the previous year. The Foreign Office insists on a British citizen performing the autopsy, whilst hoping that Laos's own Greek-Cypriot ancestry will placate the local police force. Against the beautiful backdrop of a Mediterranean summer, an undercurrent of vice and deceit simmers, and Laos must work against the odds to restore law and order.

Books by Matthew Malekos
Published by Ulverscroft:

PEROXIDE HOMICIDE

MATTHEW MALEKOS

SNOW WASTED
A DR KAREN LAOS NOVEL

Complete and Unabridged

ULVERSCROFT
Leicester

First published in Great Britain in 2014 by
Robert Hale Limited
London

First Large Print Edition
published 2015
by arrangement with
Robert Hale Limited
London

A catalogue record for this book is available
from the British Library.

ISBN 978–1–4448–2652–4

Published by
F. A. Thorpe (Publishing)
Anstey, Leicestershire

Set by Words & Graphics Ltd.
Anstey, Leicestershire
Printed and bound in Great Britain by
T. J. International Ltd., Padstow, Cornwall

This book is printed on acid-free paper

For Valerie Thomas,
lifelong friend.

1

Saturday 18 August, 2.45 a.m.
B6 Episkopi Garrison Outer Perimeter Road
Western Sovereign Base Area
Cyprus

Lieutenant Andrew Morrison was known to his colleagues and superiors as an example of how an officer ought to be. He epitomized the finest qualities of what the British Army expected from their ranks. The manner in which he behaved and the way that he conducted himself disclosed his military heritage to all that he met. His father had been a major general in his elder years and had encouraged, even pushed, his son to follow in his footsteps. It was inevitable really, having been a military brat his entire life, moving from one overseas base to another every few years, that Andrew too would end up in the armed service. It was in his blood, his blood and his genetics.

The qualities for which he was known and of which his colleagues spoke and praised him had therefore developed more from instinct than from any kind of great dedication to his chosen career. Given a choice, Andrew would have liked to have joined the rest of society outside of the closed ranks of the military and had secretly harboured a passion for astronomy. As a child, he had had few friends, and those that he had grown close to were soon replaced by new, unfamiliar faces as he and his family were relocated to yet another temporary home, following the dictated movements of his father's job.

Andrew had learned the skills of keeping himself to himself, relying on his own company rather than that of friends, and had passed his pre-teen years forming a sense of familiarity by looking to the night skies. Of all the constellations, his favourite had always been the Big Dipper. He had read extensively on this constellation, the largest, brightest and best known to many cultures. *Pinyin* to the Chinese, *Chum Sao* to the Vietnamese and, as a Greek-Cypriot acquaintance had recently told him, *Megali Arktos* to the Greeks. The acquaintance had laughed at Andrew as he had tried to form the words in English. *Megali*, he had learned, meant big or large and *Arktos* meant bear.

Aged twenty-four now, Andrew realized that his chance to study astronomy and attend university had passed him by. He had recently been promoted in rank from second lieutenant to lieutenant, much to his father's delight. He was still classified as an officer of the first order according to NATO rankings but, resigned as he was to the path his life had taken, could foresee a time in the not-too-distant future that he would make the next grade up on the military ladder. He planned to make the grade of captain, an officer of the second division, by the time he was thirty. As much as he found himself resenting his father for forcing upon him the life he now lived, he also found that he wanted to make him proud of his achievements. *My life could be much worse,* he reasoned to himself. He knew he'd made some bad choices since he arrived in Cyprus but hoped that he'd finally put them behind him tonight.

He realized, whilst deep in thoughts about his future, and indeed his past, that the night air held itself at a steady 32 degrees Celsius. The weather forecast had been correct, not that one really needed a forecast in the summer months. The road he was driving down was little more than a dusty track, but he knew it well from his childhood when his father had been posted in Cyprus and preferred to drive the B6 old road connecting the vicinity rather than the new A1 motorway that joined all of the Republic of Cyprus' main cities.

The sound of crickets in the undergrowth came loud and uninterrupted through the window of the Mitsubishi jeep and the Big Bear shone brightly from high above. Even with the windows open, the air hit his face hot and humid. Andrew had waited four years for a transfer from his last posting in Northern Ireland to realize his dream posting in Cyprus. His commanding officer had told him that four years was nothing, that thousands of other soldiers applied for a posting to Cyprus and that the average waiting time was six years. He had wondered, though never asked, whether his father had influenced his relatively quick move.

He had close to three years remaining in his current tour of service and planned to avail himself of every opportunity possible. He especially wanted to work with the United Nations in Nicosia, the island's capital where the international peacekeeping force maintained a difficult and fraught stand-off between the island's legitimate Greek-Cypriot government in the south and the illegal Turkish occupation in the north covering some 36 per cent of the island's total area.

He had been out this evening with some comrades and had visited an English bar in

Limassol, a thriving business and tourist city on the island's southern peninsula. Ordinarily restrained when it came to alcohol, Andrew knew that he had drunk far too much this evening and really shouldn't be driving. He knew too that he would struggle with a hangover and find it hard to wake up for Saturday's 7 a.m. start. Sticking to the B6 rather than the main highway meant that he was less likely to come across police patrol cars of either the Sovereign Base Area or the local Greek-Cypriot police force.

He had therefore taken a longer route than necessary, and had passed through villages such as Ypsonas, Kolossi and Erimi, small picturesque enclaves of both the local population and, in recent years, a high number of British ex-pats and retired servicemen. The relationship between the British bases and the government of the Republic of Cyprus had been somewhat strained for several years. The Republic's election of a communist president in 2008 had reignited the debate that had been ongoing since the early 1960s when Cyprus had won independence from British control.

Political tensions and sensibilities had come to a climax in early 2013 with a nationwide financial meltdown and a new conservative president, who had tried to sell

5

the idea of a unified European Union to the electorate; which had backfired when the European Union had attempted to levy a tax on individual saving accounts, a move that had angered thousands and resulted in closer ties with Russia. The tensions were palpable and daily riots had started to erode the financial gains of tourism.

The British showed no signs of giving up the ninety-six square miles that constituted its Sovereign Base Area, and the Greek-Cypriot government showed few signs of ceasing from campaigning for the return of the land the bases covered to its rightful owner: the Republic itself. Andrew had been warned by his commanding officer, as were all new arrivals to the island, to stay out of trouble and not to enrage the local population. There had been the high-profile and unsolved murder the year before Andrew arrived of a young British soldier. The British administration had sought witnesses from the local community; the local community had been unforthcoming. Blame had been speculative at best, evidence scarce, with both communities seeking to assign culpability to the other.

The diesel-fuelled engine of the bases' Mitsubishi chugged slowly and deeply as Andrew changed gears, switching to four-wheel drive mode as the road became less steady and the white chalk terrain gave way on either side to the ocean far below. He figured that he had about two metres of safe space either side of him and that within fifteen minutes he would come upon the main entrance to the base. He could see the lights from the garrison in the distance, flickering in the ghostly haze of the previous day's scorching sunshine, which had climbed to 44 degrees.

His right foot pushed hard at the accelerator, forcing fuel through the engine as the vehicle struggled to climb a small, rocky hill. As the jeep made it over the top of the incline, Andrew slowed his speed. He cleared his eyes with his hands as he looked towards the lights emanating from the base, sure that he had seen another light, less bright, coming from a distance of about twenty metres away. He looked harder. There it was again. He stopped the jeep at the top of the slope, braking so as to avoid a rough and unpleasant descent down the other side. He dimmed the headlights and looked again. The light flashed alone from the path that lay ahead. Andrew opened the driver's door and stepped out. The light came closer from the hill and he could see now that it was accompanied by the silhouette of a person. He called out, loudly.

'Hello, who are you?'

His own words echoed momentarily.

No answer.

The crickets continued their night-time chorus. *The sound of summer.* The light moved slowly up the rocky path, now no more than ten metres from where Andrew stood at the side of the jeep. He started to feel slightly uneasy as the silhouette came closer. He could hear a deep, laboured breathing and light footsteps against the dusty track. As the figure came into the dimmed headlights of the jeep, Andrew breathed a sigh of relief as he saw that the person was simply an old lady, stooped in stature, dressed in traditional black mourning robes and carrying a small lantern. Andrew didn't know the Greek language and hoped that the old lady approaching him would be able to speak English. The old lady stopped a distance of a metre from where he stood and raised the lantern to her chest.

Unable to see her face, Andrew moved in closer and saw that she was wearing a large, dark hood. For the first time since he had breathed his sigh of relief, it struck him how odd it was for an elderly lady to be out alone in the middle of this terrain at three in the morning.

'Are you OK?' he asked.

The old lady looked at him and spoke with

a low voice; her English was patchy and she sounded gruff as she formulated her words, pausing between each.

'I think I am lost. Can you help me?' she asked, her face still obscured by the dark of the night and her dark hood.

Andrew thought that he could make out the features of tanned and wrinkled skin as he tried to look at her face more closely. Her eyes didn't seem to meet his and held an odd position either side of where her nose would have been visible in the daylight.

'Where do you live?' he replied, feeling somewhat unsettled by this late-night encounter.

He shook his head gently to try to wake himself from this surreal experience and clear the clouds of alcohol and humidity from his mind. The old lady lifted her lantern and indicated a location back down the rocky hill he had just climbed. Andrew looked in the direction she had suggested. He saw nothing. His recall told him that Erimi was the closest village and that was a good twenty minutes' drive from where he and the old lady stood now. *How the hell did she get out here alone?* The thought came to his mind as he realized that something was wrong about this situation. He quickly reasoned that he had had a long and heavy night and that the sooner he helped the old lady, the sooner he would be able to get back to the base and, more importantly, his bed.

'Do you live in Erimi?' His voice pressed through the darkness.

The old lady nodded and again shook her lantern in that direction. Andrew moved to the back passenger door of the jeep and opened it, indicating with an open-arm gesture for the old lady to climb in. She moved slowly and Andrew thought he heard a metallic noise coming from under her black-as-the-night robes. She whispered what sounded like 'thank you' as she climbed into the back of the jeep.

Andrew got back in the driver's seat and, keen for this experience to come to an end, started the engine of the jeep and hit reverse. The jeep trudged slowly back down the hill, moving at no more than 10 mph, the sound of the diesel engine running heavy and amplified against the silence from the inside of the vehicle. As the jeep reached the bottom of the hill, Andrew moved his glance from the rear-view mirror he had used to navigate his way back down the hill and got ready to change gear again. He thought that he caught a glimpse of the old lady moving her hands into her gown as he stole the last seconds of his glance into the mirror. He let out a deep scream of shock and panic as the old lady lunged from the back seat and whacked him hard across the head with a foot length of metallic pole.

As Andrew slumped over into the passenger seat to his left, he felt a deep pit of bile and vomit coming up from his stomach. His vision hazy, he saw the old lady coming at him again with a noose of rope. The pain of the assault left him immobilized, his legs awkwardly limp between the two front seats, his head lodged between the passenger seat and left-side door. Unable to move and with his consciousness fading, Andrew saw the old lady reach to her face and pull at the sides of her cheeks. Her face appeared to fall away as Andrew realized in those terrifying seconds that this was no old lady at all. A young male of no more than his own age now looked down at Andrew with the wrinkled mask of an old woman held in his left hand.

With what sounded like an Eastern European accent, the man said, 'This is what happens when you don't do what you're told. You should have been a good boy, Andrew; you've pissed off the wrong people this time. We're gonna fuck you and all your mates over this time.'

He was yanking Andrew's head and forcing the rope noose around his neck, pulling tighter every half a second. He couldn't answer the man and it was then that Andrew felt his ears filling with blood and noticed his vision disappearing completely. As his consciousness left him, Lieutenant Andrew Morrison had the strange thought that the face of the young man now emblazoned indelibly into his mind was one that he recognized from earlier in the night. In the last moments of his life, he also realized exactly what his killer had been talking about.

2

Dr Karen Laos moved through her apartment steadily, a large cup of filter coffee in her right hand and a book grasped in her left, heading to her sizeable bedroom veranda overlooking Mariner's Canal. She had taken today off work. She had left her workplace, the Manchester inner-city mortuary, in the capable hands of her equally qualified colleague, Dr Ferguson. She knew he would be ably assisted today by her own understudy, Maxwell, who had now entered the trainee programme for mortuary assistants. She had watched his development as an assistant over the past few years and had personally recommended him to the city's forensic pathology training programme. Back in her own days as a student, things were very different, of course. She had entered the profession by studying medicine, the standard route back in the 1970s.

By virtue of Maxwell's accumulated hours

13

of experience working with Dr Laos, he had been accepted on an apprenticeship and hoped to become a pathologist in his own right one day. Although not academically gifted, his practical common sense and kind manner had matured in the years he had worked with Dr Laos. She had been pleased to recommend him personally for professional training.

It wasn't often that Dr Laos afforded herself the time or opportunity for relaxation, as any of her friends or colleagues would confirm. She had, however, found herself changing somewhat over the past year. Rather than spending all day, every day over the desk of her office at the mortuary, she now dedicated one evening a week for social activities. She had even dated again over the past twelve months. *So, it didn't work out with Detective Inspector James Roberts*, she reasoned quietly. Still, she had learned a great deal from him about how to separate work from her personal life and she considered him to be a close friend. With this in mind, she had also taken up reading, for enjoyment's sake, not purely for academic and educational purposes, as had always been the case previously.

Dr Laos made herself comfortable in a summer chair on her veranda and was grateful that the weather was, today at least, warm and sunny. Manchester was usually a very wet city, so she felt her timing for a day of annual leave was perfect. Instinctively, she checked her cell-phone for messages and emails. As the lead forensic pathologist at the mortuary, she was essentially on call twenty-four hours a day. Learning to delegate had been a difficult yet ultimately rewarding experience for her. She sipped on her coffee, one of only a very few regular vices she allowed herself to enjoy.

Despite having checked her cell-phone, she really hoped that today it would remain quiet, as she had by now started and stopped the same novel six times due to constant interruption. She was reading a work of fiction, a story of love lost and ultimately reclaimed. It hadn't been her choice of reading material, but one of her colleagues had suggested that she give it a go and lose herself in the story as it evolved. *If I can learn to date, I can learn to enjoy a fiction*, she had said, when agreeing to give this book a try.

Try as she did, however, Karen Laos found herself reading and again rereading the same paragraph time and time again as she sat with the sun shining on her face. Her mind was elsewhere: *back in the damn office*. There hadn't been any particularly disturbing cases

15

recently in the mortuary that would explain why she couldn't disconnect herself from work, other than run-of-the-mill deaths by natural causes, frequent car accident victims — a cause of death she felt particularly touchy about — and the usual number of inner-city suicides to which she had become accustomed. Therefore, Karen assumed that she just wasn't particularly enthralled by the book she was reading.

She closed it yet again, and sipped on her coffee. Just as she was deciding whether or not to return to her book, the sound of her cell-phone ringing made the choice for her. The name flashing across the screen was that of her regional boss for forensic pathology, Professor Michael Ogilvy. It wasn't often that he called Karen directly; she dealt with the day-to-day running of the city forensic team; he dealt with the overall management of the county and regional aspects of the pathology service. Other than meeting for clinical supervision and the occasional conference, they rarely spoke. He trusted Karen's work implicitly and she knew that he wouldn't be calling unless it were for something important. *Especially on my day off.*

She flicked her phone open and answered his call.

'Karen,' he started. 'I'm sorry to bother

16

you on your day off, but a rather interesting case has come up. I thought I should tell you about it.'

He paused, expecting Karen's response. It was forthcoming.

'Don't tell me, Michael,' she joked, 'you have the case of a lifetime for me?'

She knew her words were probing.

'Maybe not the case of your lifetime,' retorted Professor Ogilvy. 'But it could be the case of the year, if you're interested in it.'

Karen leaned into the table where the remnants of her filter coffee sat in a now nearly cold mug. She picked it up and sipped before responding.

'Tell me about it,' she said, her curiosity piqued.

'Well, the Foreign Office have issued a general appeal for a Consultant Forensic Pathologist to attend the apparent murder of a young British soldier who was stationed on the island of Cyprus, at one of the Sovereign Base Areas on the south of the island. I was emailed a copy of the Foreign Office's request this morning and immediately thought of you.'

Karen suspected she knew why. Her surname, *Laos*, clearly had Greek origins and, although it wasn't something she had discussed with Professor Ogilvy previously,

17

she knew that he would have been smart enough to pick up on this fact.

'If I'm not mistaken, Michael,' she said, 'the Sovereign Bases on the island have a fully equipped hospital and medical staff. Why would the Foreign Office be asking for a pathologist unconnected to the bases to get involved?'

'My understanding, Karen, is that due to the political tensions on the island and the generally increased tensions in the region, the facility at Episkopi Garrison is hard pushed for staff at the best of times. The conflict in the neighbouring Middle East has meant that the Ministry of Defence has had to redirect a lot of the regional staff elsewhere. Other than a handful of military medical staff, including emergency doctors and nurses, they have no permanent pathologist based there.'

Karen contemplated his explanation.

'In that case, why don't they ask for a local pathologist to get involved on this one?' she asked.

'Government protects its right to maintain the bases under a clause of sovereignty and it's a right that they have been clinging onto since Cyprus gained its independence from the UK in 1960. Also, Karen, this case is an eyes and ears only matter for the Foreign

Office. This isn't the first murder of a British military serviceman on the normally peaceful island. There was another, which was left unsolved, a little over a year ago. The diplomatic fallout was contained last time, mainly because the Greek-Cypriot government and the British administration agreed to stop blaming one another for the murder. However, as a result, no perpetrator was identified and hence no justice was forthcoming. The fact that a second British soldier has been killed in what appears, at first sight, to be similar circumstances, leaves the Foreign Office with few options as to how to tackle the case.'

'Michael,' replied Karen, 'a second case left unsolved wouldn't sit well with the military and I'm sure that neither the British nor the Greek-Cypriot government want an escalation on the island. Given what you've told me, and of course what I have seen in the news about the so-called recent Arab Spring and its proximity to Cyprus, the last thing either side wants right now is a further escalation in the region.'

'Spot on,' replied the professor. 'Such instability has also increased the island's nationalistic tendencies, with the local population having recently voted far more right-wing than in any other time in living memory. This means that inter-communal tensions are rising, along with immigration from Eastern Europe, which isn't sitting well with the local population, which is itself struggling with record high levels of unemployment and bankruptcy. The Foreign Office have made it perfectly clear that they want a British citizen involved in this; you're one of the best pathologists we have and your skills have been noted higher up on the ladder than either you or I have any involvement.'

A wave of heat crossed Karen's face and she felt herself blushing.

The professor continued, 'Karen, your name has also been flagged up.'

I knew this would be a matter of interest, Karen thought.

'My surname, Michael? Is that what you're referring to?'

'Yes,' he said, flatly.

'My paternal grandfather was Greek-Cypriot but I have no Greek language skills whatsoever, if that's what you were thinking,' she said, equally flatly.

'Actually, Karen, that isn't why. Besides, there are plenty of officers who have been on the base for a long time that speak Greek and of course local civilian personnel. It's more to do with image projection. Having a British pathologist on the case who has connections

20

to the local population, however sparse and removed they may be, is something that the Foreign Office believe will help to placate the local police if they get involved, which from my perspective is inevitable.'

The professor's words made sense. Karen quickly did her mental calculations before responding. *It would certainly be an interesting adventure. The book I have been reading isn't exactly living up to expectations. There is nothing important to keep me here in the short term. Why don't I go and see what this is all about?* A further fleeting thought simultaneously passed her mind. *Am I really such a workaholic?*

Before she had the chance to answer her own query, she found herself agreeing to Professor Ogilvy's request.

'When would I have to travel?' she asked.

'Immediately,' came the professor's response. Karen had only travelled once in her life to Cyprus and that was several years ago, despite her heritage. She knew that she had some distant family living on the island still, but her own branch of the Laos clan had long been absent from the island.

'Am I to make my own arrangements to travel, Michael?' she asked. She remembered her last trip to Cyprus. She had flown for a week's holiday with an old friend on a five-hour Cyprus Airways flight out of London Heathrow to Larnaca. She then remembered the stifling heat and that had been only in June. August would be far hotter. She shuddered as she thought about the extreme heat.

'I simply need to reply with your personal details and passport number to the Foreign Office and they will make arrangements for you to fly out from a military base as soon as you're approved. I have your details already from HR, plus of course your updated, enhanced Criminal Records Bureau checks. I suggest you pack your bags, Karen, as the Foreign Office will make the arrangements very quickly.'

Karen stood up as if her travel were imminent, and moved through the veranda doors, back into her apartment. She carried her mobile, now on hands-free, and empty coffee cup, leaving the book, still unread, on the veranda table.

'OK,' she said. 'All noted, Michael. Do you know who will contact me?'

'I have just one name, Karen, and that is of the commanding officer at Episkopi Garrison. His name is Air Vice-Marshal David Littleton. I assume it will be him that you will take your instructions from when you arrive, as well as of course receiving debriefing from any junior medical staff that have the body of the victim, awaiting your arrival. You will also work with the police involved in the case. This is where it might get more complex, as the area where the body was found falls under the Sovereign Bases jurisdiction; whilst the British police take primary responsibility for the law of the bases area, they also cooperate with the local Cypriot police force. I am simply guessing at this point but from what I have heard about the first murder, it won't be long before they also need to get involved. Be careful, Karen, and have a good trip and please check your emails later in the day. I will send you over your flight information as soon as it comes to me from the Foreign Office.'

With that, Professor Michael Ogilvy ended the call, leaving Karen to face a day ahead that was far from that which she had expected an hour earlier, when she had sat down to read her book in the sunshine on her veranda.

3

Sergii Filatov walked confidently through the busy intersection joining Marikas Kotopouli Street to Ifestou Avenue in the southern district of Nicosia. He was a tall, broad man who seemed to lurch from step to step with a jet-black thick head of hair, cut close to his ears, almost framing his face.

This was a man who walked with a purpose and a confidence that oozed arrogance from deep within. He had moved to Cyprus from his native Russian homeland during the late 1980s, a time long before the island had joined the European Union. Like many others who had moved at the time with him, Sergii and his family had long-standing roots to the communist politics that linked Cyprus and his homeland. Over the last two decades, Sergii had seen the Russian influence wax and wane as the years passed.

The initial large numbers of migrating

Russians had dissipated slightly in the 1990s as the Cypriot government of the time had prepared itself for European integration and started to develop human rights and Western models of governance, decriminalizing homosexuality and cutting down on human trafficking. The island had been successful in 2004 in achieving full membership of the European Union, and as a result thousands of Sergii's fellow Russian residents had left the island, with jobs being prioritized for European Union citizens. Sergii had been on the island long enough to know how to stay put. This was a man who would not easily give up all that he had worked so hard for.

Now in his late forties, Sergii had managed to accumulate a vast wealth for himself on this small island in the eastern Mediterranean. Capitalizing on Russian money brought into Cyprus by Sergii and others like him, he had exploited the political situation on the divided island nation by importing and selling illicit drugs and narcotics. He remembered the first days after he had moved from Russia. Both his parents had been killed, along with his siblings, in gang warfare back in Russia, and Sergii had volunteered to join a munitions ship that was chartered by the Chinese and destined for Iran.

The vessel had ultimately been detained in the waters outside of Limassol, as Sergii had hoped it would be. In order to avoid arrest, Sergii and seven others who had travelled from Russia on the vessel had decided to make the difficult and potentially dangerous journey to Limassol's shores by swimming from the vessel in the dead of the night from its anchorage position. A distance of one thousand metres had been successfully crossed by all but one of their group, who had succumbed to some nasty tidal swells. Sergii had arrived ashore exhausted in a little over an hour, in just the shorts and T-shirt that he had swum in.

He had spent the first few days of his arrival living on a remote beach that he had hiked to from where he had come ashore. He had finally ventured out into Limassol's old town and within a matter of days had managed to ingratiate himself with the local Cypriot mafia. Although his English was poor and his Greek non-existent at that time, he had quickly earned the respect of the underground mafia, earning the nickname of Sergii the Slaughterman. He was cruel and efficient in his use of terror and fear. His face still showed the scars of countless raids on local bars and clubs, where he and the gang that he worked with would persuade landlords to part with their cash in return for protection.

The Bulgarians had come a few years later, and Sergii had fought hard to protect his section of Limassol's busy tourist district, learning too how to capitalize on young holidaymakers, forcing them to part with their cash in return for trips to the rapidly emerging clubbing resort of Ayia Napa on the east coast. Once there, they would be singled out as vulnerable, and forced into smuggling drugs among their fellow revellers, often taking them to the point of insolvency. The fact that many had ended up in jail and in need of the help of the British Embassy had not fazed Sergii whatsoever. After all, for every one that he lost to the police, there would be a dozen more arriving on the next plane.

Sergii's criminal world flourished with its ties to the corrupt elements of the local police, but it was all kept deeply secret. He learned that money had influence but that it was not all-powerful in its own right. He needed the blind eye of the local law. They were happy to provide it; for a price. Much happier than they were these days. He had reached a point in his life where he was happy to rest up slightly. He was the owner of a coffee shop in Nicosia that disguised his other, less than legal, pursuits. He was meeting this morning with a man he had been doing business with for almost two years. He had called his coffee shop Kali's, quite liking the bastardization of the Greek *Kali* from *Kalimera*, for good-morning, and the mythical Indian Goddess, Kali, goddess of destruction.

Sergii didn't have much regard for anyone in particular, and trusted nobody in general. His relatively new business partner was a man of a similar age to himself, of English-Cypriot origin, who spoke with a deep cockney accent. Whilst Sergii kept a tight leash on his patch in Limassol, he was happy to listen to Charlie Charalambos' ideas regarding expansion. Sergii considered Charlie to be far less humane than he liked to think of himself.

Charlie was cut-throat in his approach to business, straight to the point and, had Sergii not commanded the level of respect he had over the years, Charlie wouldn't have paused in decimating his wealth and empire. Where Sergii sat back and left his business in the day-to-day hands of much younger criminals he had personally selected and groomed, Charlie was still very much involved in his own realm of corruption and delinquency.

Sergii preferred to live in Nicosia and keep the majority of his business in Limassol. He had been wise enough to stay out of Nicosia where the Turkish battled with the Greeks to control their own respective patches. Turf war was frequent. Sergii found it far too messy. Charlie had presented some interesting ideas, which had so far proved to be quite rewarding. He had tried to expand his own small empire from the town of Paphos on the west coast and had almost encroached upon Sergii's Limassol patch. It was at that point that the two had agreed to stick to their own sectors respectively, each acutely aware of the other's standing. They had figured it better to work together than fight; if Sergii and Charlie were to turn on one another, the Greeks and the Turks would soon take control of their respective empires and all their years' hard work would come to mean nothing.

As Sergii walked through the front door of his own coffee shop, he paused as always to check the dozen or so small tables that spread out in an arch shape in front of him. Irina, his long-term waitress, quickly scuttled out from behind the bar on the far side of the café, greeting her boss and gesturing to him to join her at a table. He nodded good morning but declined her offer. He knew as well as she did that Irina didn't really seek his company: it was simply expected that she invite her paymaster to join her every time he walked in. Keeping up appearances or, as Irina told her friends, keeping a job and therefore an income. Even if it meant that she was working for the Devil. Irina went back to her tasks of cleaning tables and placing menus in readiness for the lunchtime rush that was always inevitable after midday.

Two dozen businessmen would descend on the small coffee shop, most of whom were genuinely in the dark about the owner's secret life and other business pursuits. A couple, by virtue of being locals, had come to know Sergii over the years. Cyprus was still a small island and in many ways everyone knew each other; a distant friend may turn out to be the husband of your second cousin. Gossip in particular spread fast. It was for this reason that Sergii walked through the coffee shop and headed up a spiral staircase to his office.

Charlie would arrive shortly through the back door and Irina would show him upstairs, where Charlie would, as always, turn every word into an unnecessary sentence, each one sure to be laced with self-aggrandizing sentiments and overly exaggerated statements. The trouble with Charlie was that he had crossed so many lines in his life that most people wouldn't even dream about, that Sergii never knew whether he was telling the truth or bullshitting his way out of an awkward situation. Charlie, although a good colleague and interesting acquaintance, had long ago crossed the thin line between madness and sanity. He seemed to lurk now forever in the blurry junction between the two, three-quarters of his body, including his head, in the realms of insanity and the remaining quarter somehow anchored in a state that resembled sanity.

Sergii rapped his watch and turned on his PC as he waited for Charlie's arrival. He was eager to find out how it had gone down with the soldiers from the British bases. That was one market previously untapped and one which Sergii wanted.

Monday 20 August, 11.45 a.m.
Central Command
Episkopi Garrison
Western Sovereign Base Area
Cyprus

Air Vice-Marshal David Littleton had been one of two commanding officers for both Episkopi and Akrotiri bases, which fell together under the Western Sovereign Base Area, for a total of seven years. Littleton's position was a two-star rank belonging to the British Royal Air Force. It was a position that alternated every three years between the British Army and the British Royal Air Force. His counterpart, the Deputy British Forces Cyprus, a one-star rank from the British Army, had been on extended leave for several months. Currently in command, David Littleton felt a little uncomfortable about the prospect of his reliever returning later in the year. The system of a two-star commander alternating with a one-star commander from the opposite service had long been common practice on the island as a means of enabling both Royal Air Force and Army officers to share the responsibility.

In the years that David Littleton had been stationed here, he had come to both respect and admire the island of Cyprus. He didn't always feel safe and was acutely aware of the island's many political and economic difficulties. Still, he understood why so many ex-servicemen had chosen to settle on the island. Given his position, he had little freedom over his own personal comings and goings but pictured a time when he would be able to move more freely. Littleton was considered to be a humane yet redoubtable soldier and military strategist with an impressive wealth of experience under his belt.

His previous command had been in Beirut, only twenty-five minutes' flight time from the southern tip of Cyprus. He found life on the island much more peaceful than he had in Lebanon. He knew that six years in command of a base was longer than normal and felt pleased to have been given the opportunity to continue in his current post. However, now in his mid-60s and voluntarily working past his retirement age, David knew that it would be only a matter of time before his superiors in London put him out to pasture. That was not a thought that he liked to entertain. He quickly pushed it from his mind.

He sat firmly back into his desk chair and lifted a bundle of paperwork from in front of him. The air conditioning remained at a steady 17 degrees Celsius. He cringed as he thought about the recent tragic events that had resulted in the death of Lieutenant Andrew Morrison. Morrison had been a good soldier and his father had been a good friend of David's for many years. A twang of guilt quickly struck him as he remembered Andrew as a young child. He had been a happy, if somewhat distant kid. A small voice in his head came to life as he thought about Andrew Morrison. *You deserve more than just a twang of guilt, David*, it opined against his conscious will.

He brushed it aside. When David had heard that Andrew had joined the military he hadn't been at all surprised. Andrew's father was a formidable character and David knew that Andrew would have had little choice with regard to his own career path. The twang of guilt returned as he recalled telling Major General Morrison that he would 'take care' of his son when he had commenced his duties on the island. David Littleton again rebuked the sense of guilt, knowing as he did that the coming days were bound to be difficult at best. He lifted a single page of A4 paper and read the heading, *Doctor Karen Laos, Consultant Forensic Pathologist*. The faxed résumé had arrived in his office an hour ago. He scanned the brief information on the page now held in his hands. Dr Laos certainly had a notable résumé and some very strong references, available if required. The Air Vice-Marshal reached for his pen and signed the approval, adding the date and time as he checked his watch. He stamped the official seal of the Sovereign Bases Authority and prepared to send the document back to the Foreign Office in London. Although his signature and stamp had been required, Littleton knew it was no more than a formal procedure in paper exercise.

The decision to bring Dr Karen Laos to Cyprus had been made already by people far higher up in the military, sitting in the shadowy offices of the Foreign Office in London. *Two bodies of two young soldiers found within little more than a year of one another, both on my watch,* Littleton thought to himself. He hadn't liked the fact that the first murder had been left unsolved but had bowed to political pressure from both London and the Republic of Cyprus. He now secretly hoped that Dr Karen Laos would be able to bring some sense of order to the whole mess and provide some closure to the families of both soldiers.

As long as she stays out my hair. Littleton knew that family members of military personnel accepted the risks that came with military deployment but he also knew that death by a seemingly senseless murder summoned no sense of honour or conclusion. He reasoned to himself that Dr Laos would be in Cyprus by late evening. She would certainly have a lot of work to do during her stay, however long that might turn out to be.

He also knew that retired Major General Morrison would soon be on his way to the base with his wife to collect their son's body for repatriation to the UK. Repatriation would depend entirely on Dr Laos' opinion and she wouldn't be releasing the body until she had concluded her investigations to her satisfaction.

4

Charlie Charalambos was a short man with a wiry and near-frantic appearance, strongly generated by the way in which he thought about the world. He had come from a large, wealthy East London family of Greek-Cypriot heritage and had rebelled against his grandparents' strong Orthodox faith. Frequently in trouble as a child and often expelled from school, Charlie had been subjected to a violent teenage gang culture in London's East End. His taste for narcotics had developed in the back of friends' cars and in the toilets of the very schools where he should have been receiving his education.

As he walked into Kali's Café in Laiki Yitonia village, Sergii's employee, Irina, shuddered and felt a cold chill moving down her spine. She knew what would come next. Sure enough, Charlie moved in her direction

37

and embraced her, kissed her on both cheeks and let his right hand move up and down her back; lower down her back than she found comfortable. She forced a friendly smile, aware as she was that this was not a man that liked to be rejected. He had, other than the occasional grope here and there, been respectful towards Irina in the years they had known one another. She moved off to behind the bar and made Charlie a latte — his favourite mid-morning beverage.

'How did you know I wanted a latte?' Charlie asked Irina, his voice somewhat suspicious.

She winked at him.

'Charlie, darling, you haven't changed your standing order in all the time I've known you.'

A smile finally came to his face. 'You're a real diamond Irina, have I ever told you that?'

Yes, you have, every goddamn day for as long as I can remember, she thought. Charlie collected his latte and headed upstairs.

By the age of fifteen, Charlie had been the cause of his parents' and grandparents' frequent arguments. A stalemate had been reached when Charlie's mother had suffered a nervous breakdown due to her son's unruly behaviour. Charlie had been told to leave the family house; his grandparents were too old and too proud in their Greek Orthodox faith to intervene on his behalf. They asked God why their grandson had turned into the destructive whirlwind that had whipped their lives up and so out of control. They had asked Mary, the Mother of God, where they had gone so wrong. They had offered a healthy slice of Greek guilt to assuage the Lord's anger.

Living on the streets had been relatively easy for Charlie. He was by then already a stranger to his own family and therefore had not spent much time in the family house for a few years. His brain was slightly affected and his thoughts random, not that he himself realized this. His taste for drugs had developed from cannabis and alcohol to cocaine and amphetamines. He had by the age of seventeen developed a taste for heroin, a substance that led him down a very dark path for the next two years that followed. He had resorted to burglary and petty crime to fund his drug habits; he had refused the assistance of the local Social Services when he fell across their radar as an adolescent in need. Down and out and with the burden of a mind warped by a plethora of drugs, Charlie had left his native East End and headed into Central London's Soho. There he had made money by turning to prostitution, as many young men had, rarely by want, and fuelled by need.

Where social services had failed to snap Charlie out of his self-destructive habits, a large black man calling himself Bob had succeeded. Bob had been more than willing to pay Charlie £5 for a blowjob in one of Soho's back alleys. What Charlie hadn't realized was that Bob was a predatory sex offender with a history of abducting the young men he paid for sexual gratification. He had snatched Charlie up, taken him to what he claimed was his flat and injected him with heroin for three days straight, sexually abusing and raping him at will. Bob had long vanished by the time that Charlie had regained consciousness. Charlie spent the next ten days in a psychiatric hospital, having entered cold turkey. He suffered terrible incontinence of bowel and bladder and had to be stabilized by lorazepam and methadone medication.

It was shortly after his discharge from hospital that Charlie decided to try to return home. His parents had been surprised to see him, pleased that he was alive but not willing to have him back in the family home. They could see something was psychologically amiss and that he had changed for the worse. They offered to put him on a plane and send him to his Uncle Andreas and Aunty Despina in Paphos. He could do little other than agree, for he had burned all of his other bridges a long time ago.

Charlie had been in Cyprus for close to twenty years. As a result of his Greek heritage he had spoken the native tongue since he was a small child. His grandparents had known little English, and Greek remained the language of choice in the family home when he was young. It came back to him relatively easily, therefore, when he had moved to the island permanently. He hadn't stayed long with his uncle and aunty. They found that their nephew was too difficult to manage.

This suited Charlie as much as it suited them in the long run; he had learned how to manipulate the same cultural Greek guilt that had affected his grandparents. He made his uncle and aunt's lives impossible until they agreed to give him a cut of their land in the mountains surrounding Paphos. He moved there when he was twenty-one years of age and started building himself a small house. He preferred living alone in the solitude of the countryside and only returned to the town when he needed money. It wasn't long thereafter before Charlie had formed his own connections with the mafia in Paphos.

They had tried to manipulate him but

having been abused and manipulated before, Charlie had taken some of the younger members of the gang by surprise by viciously putting them out of action forever. His fierce and aggressive lust for violence quickly endeared him to an aging Cypriot mafia boss, Stelios Epiphaniou, who had decided to fund his young protégé by way of lavishing him with cash and weekend breaks to Tel Aviv, Beirut and Northern Africa. Charlie's wealth grew, as Stelios harnessed his unstable personality and encouraged him with each new step that Charlie took into the realms of violence and eventually murder. By the time he was 30 years old, Charlie had Paphos' inner city and old town firmly in the grasp of his hands. Not a single restaurant, nightclub or bar had been left untouched by his rise to dominance. Pocketing a tidy quarter of the profits from all of these establishments meant that Charlie could redirect his funds into protection and extortion. It wouldn't be fair to say that Charlie was superior to his colleague Sergii; both had accumulated their own respective wealth and knew that pooling their resources would make them stronger. What they didn't realize was that there would come a point at which greed and opportunism would be the very cause of their own downfall. As they sat now looking across

Sergii's desk at one another on the top floor of Kali's Café, they were less concerned with what might be and more with what had been.

Sergii stood up, his hands behind his back, and started pacing up and down the fifteen-metre length of his office.

'Tell me, Charlie,' he said, his voice thick and heavy, 'have you been making mistakes again?'

Charlie looked up at the face of his colleague, but remained seated.

'Not me, Sergii; one of those stupid young lads took it too far.'

Sergii stopped pacing and took his seat again.

'You know what they say, Charlie: fool me once, shame on you; fool me twice, shame on me.'

He tapped his thick fingers upon his desk and pushed his gut into the wooden trim.

'These lads you're using, do you even know their names?'

Charlie's mind ticked over slowly. 'I know their nicknames, Sergii, and one I know very well but I don't probe, if that's what you mean.'

'Maybe,' replied Sergii, 'you should *start* probing before you employ their services. You know how important the British bases are to me; what was the point in our going into partnership if your boys are continually going to fuck things up?'

Charlie threw his hands in the air, clearly becoming agitated.

'I'm not the all-seeing eye, Sergii. For fuck's sake, mate, you want the bases, I'll get them for you. That's exactly what I've been trying to do since the first time you mentioned it to me.'

Sergii smiled to himself. He liked to rile his colleague's emotions. But he also knew when to calm the situation back down.

'OK Charlie, just make sure it doesn't happen again, will you? Your lads have killed two soldiers since we started this operation. The last thing either of us needs is the British cops crawling all over us.'

'Every war has casualties, Sergii, you know that as well as anyone.'

'All I'm saying, Charlie, is that if we're going to reap the rewards of our little venture we need better control over those that work for us. I see a lot of potential in the bases and I'm not saying you haven't done well. I know you've worked hard and I know too that you've got people on the inside helping us out; all I'm asking is that you make it clear to those people that if they make any more cock-ups, I won't be as forgiving as I have been up to now.'

Having enjoyed the little stroking of his ego that Sergii had given him, Charlie now sensed a surge of excitement as he thought about the rewards that would come his way. He also felt excited at the prospect of seeing Sergii kick someone's ass if he got upset. He stayed silent and waited for Sergii to continue.

Sergii's eyes had become somewhat beady as he spoke. He looked like he was about to win the lottery. Charlie liked the anticipation. Sergii knew that he was about to be regaled with predominantly fiction but had learnt how to pick the facts out of Charlie's often convoluted stories.

'Well, Sergii, I wasn't there in person; I'm too old for all that these days. The late nights do me in, but I heard from one of the lads that six of them travelled as a group to the Folk's Arms pub in Limassol, and found a group of British lads. My lads, you understand, are mostly from the Eastern Bloc but I got a couple that are British too; ruthless lads, I may add. You'd be proud of them, Sergii.'

Sergii ignored Charlie's invitation to lavish him once more with praise and waited for him to continue.

'They spotted some of the lads and got talking to them, found out they were from the bases and started doing business with them.

Apparently we've now got more than a dozen of the British soldiers dealing. They're hooked, Sergii, good and proper. But one of the boys, a young lieutenant, pissed my lads off. He said he'd had enough of drugs and all that stuff. He left alone from the pub and said he had no money to pay us back what he owed us. My lads followed him and called ahead to a mate they've got on the base. They told him where to find this guy and that's it, Sergii. He paid the price for fucking with us.'

5

Karen Laos had received an email at shortly after 9.30 a.m. from Professor Michael Ogilvy, confirming that she would indeed be heading to Cyprus to work on the investigation of the murder of Lieutenant Andrew Morrison, whose body was now being held in what Karen assumed would be a dated and makeshift military mortuary at Episkopi Garrison. *Will they have all the tools I will need to conduct a thorough investigation?* She had found herself contemplating such thoughts as she sat in the back of the military taxi that had come to collect her from her apartment at exactly 11 a.m. She had therefore had three hours to make herself ready to travel at such short notice.

Fortunately Karen — being as efficient as always — had managed to pack her suitcase and finalize some last-minute details in less than an hour and a half. She had allowed herself some extra time to make notes on the

47

constitution of the Sovereign Bases. She wanted to know what to expect when she landed and commenced her temporary duties on the island. She had learnt a great deal with the help of Google and Wikipedia. She knew already that the British had a total of four separate bases spread across the island. Two fell under the Eastern Sovereign Base Area, in Dhekalia and Ayios Nikolaos. The remaining two comprised Akrotiri and Episkopi Garrison, under the auspices of the Western Sovereign Base Area.

It was in Episkopi Cantonment that Karen's interest lay as it was there that she would be landing late this evening and starting her work. Feeling full of unanswered questions and slightly unsettled by the quick turn of events that the day had delivered to her, Karen Laos felt that the least she could do was to read more about the bases and their roles and functions, knowing this would help her answer some queries she had. She assumed that the more important answers would be found upon her arrival in Cyprus.

Karen had not, for example, realized that the bases, when taken as a whole, formed a separate British Overseas Territory in their own right and that individuals born on the bases were not automatically entitled to full British citizenship, being granted instead the slightly lower classification of a British Overseas Territories Citizenship, an unusual mark of identity solely reserved for the bases in Cyprus.

What intrigued Karen more, however, was the political and civilian disagreement, which had been longstanding with the Republic of Cyprus itself. The bases were retained by the British, under a 1960 Treaty of Independence, which had been agreed and signed by the UK, Greece, Turkey and representatives of both the Greek and Turkish Cypriot communities and granted independence to the then Crown colony of Cyprus. Karen learned that the controversy over the legality of the British right to continue using their bases for military purposes on the island, close to the Suez Canal and the Middle East in general, had been an issue that had hampered the Republic of Cyprus' relationship with the UK over the last five decades.

The political situation on the island made a lot more sense to Karen after she had read that following the 1974 Turkish invasion of Northern Cyprus, neither Britain nor Greece had honoured the Treaty of Guarantee, which had established the two countries, along with Turkey, as having guaranteed powers of the Republic of Cyprus.

Karen checked her watch and saw the

time approaching 3.20 p.m. The drive from Manchester had been relatively straightforward and the driver had covered the 100-mile distance in a little over two hours. Another entire hour was wasted on simply getting into RAF Cranwell, where she now sat waiting for her flight at 5 p.m. She hadn't felt intimidated by the security measures through which she had to pass to get into the base but simply tired; not only from the taxi ride but by the thought of the plane journey that lay ahead.

Five hours, give or take, depending on air traffic and weather conditions across Western and Central Europe, wasn't a long flight by any stretch of the imagination. She simply found it tedious and would rather have been travelling with company. She had never flown in a military plane before and therefore wasn't too sure what to expect. She half expected to be ushered into a plane with little seating room and had images of planes from the television series *M.A.S.H.* — she laughed at her own perception but couldn't picture anything else. She would land in Cyprus at approximately midnight local time. She looked around the room in which a young soldier had told her to take a seat.

The seat turned out to be no more than a stretch of a wooden bench that expanded along four square walls. There was little ventilation and just two small, high windows out of which she could not see anything other than clouds in the sky above. A small desk sat in the centre of the room, unmanned as yet, and a large metallic door on the far side from where Karen sat indicated the exit. She stood up to stretch her legs and walked towards the unmanned desk. On it she found a pile of information leaflets, each one entitled: *Preparing to Fly: A Passenger's Guide to the Hercules C1/3.*

Karen assumed that the Hercules C1/3 was the plane on which she would be travelling to Episkopi. She picked up one of the leaflets and opened it. It had only a few pages of printed information within. She took it and walked back to the rather uncomfortable wooden bench. She sat back down and opened the first page of the leaflet. There she saw a coloured photograph of the Hercules C1/3. *It's pretty grey,* was all she could think on first inspection.

She turned the first page and scanned the text that greeted her.

Welcome aboard. The C-130 Hercules tactical transport aircraft is the workhorse of the RAF's Air Transport (AT) fleet and is based at RAF Brize Norton, in Oxfordshire, and RAF Cranwell, in Lincolnshire, where it is operated by Number 24, 30, 47, and 70 Squadrons. The fleet totals 50 aircraft and is a mixture of C1/C3 aircraft and the new C-130J aircraft, designated C4/C5.

Karen paused and tried to remember her last trip aboard the Cyprus Airways flight. She recalled that there had been a screen in the back of the seat in front of her that had computerized information that told her the journey from Heathrow to her destination, then in Larnaca, was 3,200 km. She remembered the friend she had travelled with back then telling her that scheduled flights with Cyprus Airways always took slightly longer than chartered airlines, or indeed British Airways scheduled flights, because they were not allowed to pass over Turkish airspace.

She diverted her eyes back to the page in front of her, pulling herself out of recollection. *The freight bay can accommodate a range of wheeled or tracked vehicles, or up to seven pallets of general freight. In the aeromedical evacuation role either 64 or 82 stretchers can be carried, depending on the make of aircraft and the stretcher configuration. The maximum unrefuelled ferry range is 3,500 nmls, which can be extended to over 4,000 nmls by air-to-air refuelling. The other main role of the C-130 is Transport Support*

(TS), which is the airborne delivery of personnel or stores by airdrop.

Karen wondered whether she would be considered under the classification of airborne personnel; she certainly didn't want to be airdropped. *I'm simply a passenger,* she assured herself.

In this role, the aircraft supports airborne operations conducted by 16 Air Assault Brigade by the aerial delivery of paratroops, stores and equipment.

Just as Karen was about to turn the page, her attention was distracted to the door through which she had passed on her way in. She heard it open and saw two older people walking in; a male and a female. Karen couldn't quite place their ages but guessed that they were probably in their late sixties, maybe in their early seventies. The old man was dressed in military fatigues and the old woman, whose hand he held in his own, kept her head low and wore a formal green dress and faux-fur coat. They both made their way to the bench that lined the wall directly across from where Karen was sitting.

The old man formed a tired but kindly smile in Karen's direction and she reciprocated. His companion didn't look up and Karen thought that her face looked full of grief. She was certainly preoccupied. They sat down on the wooden bench, their hands still wrapped together. Karen assumed that the man worked for the military: his clothing gave a lot away. She was about to avert her gaze back to the leaflet on the Hercules when the door opened again. This time, a small group of young soldiers walked in. Karen studied them individually, and placed them in their early twenties. One of them seemed even younger and Karen thought he looked as if he still belonged in school.

They were making lots of noise and acting immaturely. They hadn't seen the older man sitting against the far wall. Karen watched as he stood up from the bench, uncupping his companion's hands from his own, and started walking in the direction of the young soldiers. One of the soldiers, the tallest of the group, stopped talking and signalled to his colleagues to do the same. A silence louder than the noise they had just been making befell the room as the old man's footfalls echoed around the walls. He walked upright, proud and with purpose. As he closed in on the group, they all turned in his direction and, as if in slow motion, one by one noticed his uniform and military insignia, which Karen had previously failed to spot. Not that she would have understood its meaning. She watched as each member of the small group of young soldiers raised their hands and saluted the old man.

He told them that they were at ease and looked at the tallest member of the group.

'Lieutenant,' he said with a voice that spoke quietly but sounded full of explosive threat, recognizing the young man's own rank, 'is there any particular reason why you and your friends have to shout and make such a spectacle of yourselves?'

The young soldier looked somewhat ashamed of himself. He stepped forward, his eyes fixed dead ahead but avoiding looking into the old man's eyes directly.

'Sir,' he said, robotically. 'I apologize to you, Major General. We are simply feeling excited about being posted to Cyprus, sir. We should have been more careful.'

Major General, Karen thought. *That's why he's dressed like that.* She couldn't help but watch as the conversation developed.

'Excitement, young man, is quite acceptable. However, when you're dressed in that uniform we expect and require certain standards of professionalism. I'm sure that you don't want me to have to ask your CO to remind you of what those standards are — do you?'

'No, sir, that is not necessary.'

Karen felt slightly sorry for the young man.

None of his companions had said a single word to help him out of an obviously awkward situation.

'Good,' said the major general. 'There is something else you will have to learn, young man. It is something called intuition. When you enter a room where there are strangers, try to ascertain the *feel* of the setting and atmosphere before you let your mouth make such unpleasant sounds.'

He studied each soldier, individually. Each nodded but none spoke.

'You see, I am here with my grieving wife. You may all be excited about going to Cyprus but my wife and I are far from excited. Do you know why?'

The tall soldier shook his head in ignorance.

'Because, young man, we are on our way there to collect the dead body of our son who was murdered two days ago on the very same base you are so excited about landing at in about six hours' time.'

Karen felt her heart beat faster. Here she was in the very same room as the parents of the dead soldier she would soon be opening up on a gurney in a mortuary. *How do I explain who I am if he comes over to me?* she thought, feeling like she was back in primary school. The group of soldiers looked embarrassed and deflated. They each apologized in person to the major general. The old man turned back to where his wife was sitting, and started in her direction. He stopped and turned to Karen. She tried not to look at him but felt his magnetism pulling her eyes in his direction. Before she knew it, she was standing up and smiling at him.

He reciprocated.

'You don't look like a soldier, young lady,' he said softly.

'No, I am not a soldier, sir,' replied Karen. The old man looked at her curiously. Karen decided to put him out of his inquisitiveness. After all, she would have to identify herself eventually and with a five-hour flight ahead of them both where they would more than likely be forced into speaking to one another, she felt it to be the professional thing to do.

'My name is Dr Karen Laos, sir. I am a civilian forensic pathologist who happens to have been recruited by the military to do some consultancy work at the Sovereign Bases.'

The major general held his composure as he digested Karen's words. He had clearly realized the connection that he and Dr Laos now shared.

'Well, Dr Laos, I am sure that we will be

talking to one another in further detail over the coming days. I wish you a pleasant flight.'

With that, he turned and walked away briskly. Awkwardly, Karen checked her watch and saw that she still had another forty-five minutes to pass before her flight. She picked up the leaflet she had left on her bench and pretended to be interested in the technical jargon she now found herself reading and rereading to pass the time. *Why the hell didn't I bring that damn romantic novel with me?* she thought. She buried her head in the Hercules C1/3 leaflet and tried to look busy.

6

The noise emitted from the engines of the Hercules C1/3 military transport plane that Karen had been travelling in for the past five hours started to change, as the aircraft approached Cyprus from a north-westerly direction. Karen was jolted awake from a light sleep that had initially been unforthcoming during the first three hours of the flight. The background noise of the engines at high altitude had acted almost as a sedative to Karen as she had sat feeling increasingly tired throughout the flight. High-altitude engine noise was caused by compression and rarefaction of the surrounding air, which, during this flight, had been relatively peaceful. Had the skies been stormy, the movement of air particles around the plane would have caused pressure waves and hence a far less peaceful flying experience.

The aircraft felt lethargic as it began its

descent into Episkopi Garrison. As the plane continued its descent, Karen heard the aerodynamic noise from the aircraft fuselage and control surfaces increase. The noise increased more as the plane amplified its landing speed. The low altitude of the jet also meant that the density of the external air caused a great deal of additional noise. There were few windows and the interior of the plane was simple and practical. The seats, numbering fifty in total, divided across two lanes of eight seats of three and thirteen seats of two, were a dull, grey colour with a hard plastic back, reinforced only by dark-green linen. Karen noticed that a number of the seats were closer to what one would find in a drive-thru diner and worked on the basis of having to manually pull them out of the internal fuselage wall.

A few of the young soldiers that had earlier been scolded by Major General Morrison had taken those seats. The major general and his wife had been seated at the front of the plane, between the cockpit and the main cabin area. There had been six flight crew onboard and, although attentive in general, they had given a great deal of their attention to the Morrisons. A further group of soldiers had joined the flight shortly before the plane took off and, although she was not 100 per cent sure,

Karen thought that a number of military policemen had also boarded the flight. Their uniforms were different to those that she saw daily on the average street cop, and different too from those that the soldiers wore. *There is much that will become clearer when I actually land*, Karen had reassured herself.

Karen looked out of a small window that was situated slightly too high on her right side. She saw nothing until the pilot rolled the plane to the right side, bringing into view a number of lights below, which Karen averaged to be at about 200 metres beneath the plane's current trajectory. Episkopi Garrison jutted out on a peninsula that formed the coastline of Limassol and its surrounding villages. As the plane continued its descent, the sound of the propellers became more evident than it had been during flight, with external airflow passing across the blades and the wings, one of which was within reaching distance of Karen's seat.

Mechanical lights had been turned on, informing the passengers that seatbelts should remain fastened. Other than that, Karen found that she relied entirely on the aircraft's own noises and fluctuations to tell her where she was and how close they were to landing. Her own internal senses also gave her some indication of what was happening;

her ears popping as the plane descended indicated that landing was imminent.

The plane landed smoothly amid a field of runway lights stretching ahead and out to the sides. The pilot manoeuvered the plane approximately 300 metres and taxied at a hangar that Karen could make out through the window now that she had unbuckled her belt and stood up. She simply followed the actions of the other passengers. Nobody seemed at all fazed that the pilot hadn't instructed them to disembark, nor that the plane had finalized taxiing. When the doors opened, the hot air pushed its way into the cool interior of the plane's cabin.

A runway worker had moved a mobile staircase alongside the vehicle and after a short walk down sixteen steps, Karen found herself on the runway, being greeted by Air Vice-Marshal David Littleton. He was dressed informally in a short-sleeved dusky shirt and cotton trousers. Karen wouldn't have known his designation had he not stepped forward and introduced himself to her. *He either recognizes me from my résumé*, thought Karen, *or simply knows everybody else that disembarked from the aircraft and therefore singled me out from the crowd.*

Karen watched as Major General Morrison

and his wife walked off in the opposite direction. He had paused briefly to shake hands with David Littleton. Karen hadn't heard what he had said to his old friend as they both spoke inaudibly. The background noise of the airplane's engines shutting down and that of crickets also obscured their voices. A young lady stepped forward from behind Littleton. Karen hadn't seen her until she was standing only a foot away. She outstretched her hand in Karen's direction.

'Hello, Dr Laos,' she said, speaking above the noise of the plane's engines. 'My name is Rebekah Terrobias. I am a Regimental Medical Officer. I'm here to help you with your investigations.'

Karen returned the greeting and studied her new colleague's clothing. She was dressed in standard army khaki colours and beneath a dark-blue beret had blond hair pulled back into a hairgrip. The beret she wore had an emblem stitched into the fabric. The emblem depicted what looked to Karen to be a coat of arms, at the top of which stood an image of the British Crown and in the centre of which Karen identified quickly the standard, international medical image of a snake entwining a rod. Karen of course knew that this was the Rod of Asclepius. She also recognized the Latin script stitched beneath, which read 'In

Arduis Fidelis'. Karen remembered the words from her medical training: Faithful in Adversity.

'Dr Laos,' said the air vice-marshal. 'I know that the time is late and that you have had a long day but if you wouldn't mind coming with us for thirty minutes or so, we will give you a brief overview of the kind of routine we have here on the base, and of course a rundown of the case for which you have been asked to come here.'

'Of course, Mr Littleton,' Karen replied, somewhat tired but nonetheless used to late nights. 'To be honest, I would rather know more about the case, assuming of course you have any more information, as I was only briefed for a split second this morning.'

The air vice-marshal took Karen's bags from her and led her and Dr Terrobias across the runway and into a small Nissen hut that looked as if it had been standing on the same stretch of tarmac for decades. The air vice-marshal swung open a metallic screen door, adorned with a mosquito net, which led into a petite but generally tidy office. He walked to the far side and sat behind a desk, as full of paperwork and files as Karen's own desk back in Manchester, which she now felt was a million miles away.

Rebekah Terrobias pulled out two foldable

chairs and placed them on the floor so that they were facing the air vice-marshal. Karen sat in one; Rebekah sat in the other. Littleton leaned forwards and looked first at Rebekah and then at Dr Laos. Karen waited for him to speak and planned on as few interruptions as possible, having checked the clock on one of the office walls and noting that the time was quickly approaching 1 a.m.

'Dr Laos,' said Littleton, 'let me first start by saying how pleased we are to have you here with us on the team, even if the job is temporary. I have had the chance to read your résumé and I found it very impressive.'

Karen smiled her appreciation.

'However, something terrible has befallen our usually peaceful little base here. In the course of a little over one year, we have lost two young soldiers; two bright young men with equally bright futures ahead of them. As you will have heard already from your own superiors, both young men died as a result of murder.'

Karen reached into her bag for a notepad and pen. She wanted to be sure that she wouldn't miss any important details as she was feeling tired.

'Mr Littleton,' she said, feeling somewhat unsure as to whether she should address the commanding officer by his title or whether

Mr would suffice. She hadn't been told and figured that as she wasn't a soldier, it wasn't necessary for her to address him as her superior. 'What was the name of the first victim? Please can you tell me a little about the way in which he died and what happened to his body; what was the outcome?'

Littleton needed no time to recollect the details. Almost routinely he started to describe the events. 'Dr Laos, you have to understand that other than the usual politics that sometimes besiege officers and service-men on any military base, anywhere in the world, our base is a very peaceful little family of servicemen and women. I have been here six years and we never had unsolved crimes of this kind before John Riley's death — he was the first murder victim.'

Karen nodded to indicate her sympathy and that she understood Littleton's opening.

'John was a young soldier. He was twenty-two years old when he was found dead on the outskirts of the bases area.'

'What was his rank, Mr Littleton?' Karen asked.

'He was a second lieutenant, Dr Laos. He had just started his first overseas posting. He was new to Cyprus. Why do you ask?'

'I'm simply trying to draw some common denominators between the two murders. I understand that the case was left unsolved; can you tell me anything about who the pathologist was that examined Mr Riley's body?'

Littleton paused and seemed slightly uncomfortable.

'I'm afraid to say, Dr Laos, that Mr Riley's body was never inspected by a pathologist.'

'Can I ask how that was allowed, Mr Littleton?' she asked.

'To be honest with you, Dr Laos,' he replied, 'at the time of John Riley's murder, the regional tensions were extremely high. We had very few precious resources here at the bases. I admit that we made mistakes. You have to understand, the situation was out of my hands.'

He lifted his hands in the air as if to surrender.

'The Ministry of Defence wanted the case kept on a tight leash and, I hope you won't repeat this to anyone else, it was deemed more important for the sake of national and regional peace to quietly let the murder slip under the radar.'

Karen felt very uneasy about what she had been told. 'I can't imagine that Mr Riley's family were very happy about that, Mr Littleton,' she replied.

'As I said, the case was quietly and secretly

manoeuvered to fit with the MOD's plans. We were dealing not only with regional tensions and uprisings across the water in the Middle East, but we were also all still reeling from the effects of the Republic of Cyprus electorate voting a communist president to power. We had the implicit threat of Russian involvement. As for Mr Riley's family, he had no parents or siblings. He had chosen a life in the military because, I suppose, it gave him a sense of family, as it does to many of our young soldiers. He had only one maternal aunt and she died shortly after Mr Riley's own death. I believe that she was told he had died in combat.'

Karen didn't want to insult Air Vice-Marshal Littleton, but she couldn't quite believe that he had openly admitted a cover-up. It certainly wasn't how Karen planned to work. It went against all of her professional training, and her personal instincts.

'So, Mr Littleton, why on this occasion have the MOD and Foreign Office decided to properly investigate the death of the latest victim? Is it anything to do with the fact that his father is a retired major general?'

Her question was certainly loaded and she noticed that Littleton had lost his friendly and open manner. She also watched Rebekah

Terrobias recoil into the recesses of her chair.

'Dr Laos, I know what you are suggesting probably makes sense to you but I must say that I find your question offensive,' replied Littleton.

'Sir, that was not my intention, but you have to allow me the space and respect I need to be able to conduct my investigations. That is, I believe, why you asked me here?'

Littleton looked slightly defeated. 'Yes, Dr Laos. That is why we asked you here. I apologize. You shall of course have full recourse to ask the questions you think necessary. I must say, however, that it may seem suspicious that we are investigating Andrew Morrison's death when we very wrongly failed to do so for Mr Riley. I can assure you that it is pure coincidence; there is no cover-up. The timing of Andrew's death is simply more suitable for us to investigate; the previously perceived threat from the Russians has not come to pass and, although we are still low on numbers here, the Cypriot population seem as discontented with their own president as we are. In addition, although the troubles in the Middle East rumble on as always, the Arab Spring has rid us of several dictators already and the Ministry of Defence is quietly confident that the repercussions will have minimal, if any, outcome on the bases here.'

Karen wasn't feeling quite so confident as the air vice-marshal seemed to be; she had been unnerved by her first meeting with Littleton. She tried to conceal her personal feelings and concentrate on the work that lay ahead. She turned to Rebekah Terrobias.

'Dr Terrobias, I assume that you have examined Mr Morrison's body?'

Rebekah Terrobias looked somewhat embarrassed.

'Actually, Dr Laos, I have not.' She looked hesitatingly at her superior. He nodded for her to continue.

'I simply escorted the body back to the small mortuary we have here, on orders from my superiors. We have all been awaiting your arrival.'

Karen had gone past being shocked at the level of general mishandling that she had heard of in the course of her meeting with Littleton and Terrobias.

'I assume the police accompanied you when you escorted the body to the mortuary?' she asked.

Terrobias nodded. 'Yes, Dr Laos, they did.'

'Can I ask you their names?' replied Karen.

He took a pen and paper and wrote three names.

'The officers named on this piece of paper,

Dr Laos, are members of the military police. They work solely for the Sovereign Base Areas Police, who uphold all aspects of military law, along with the Cyprus Joint Police Unit.'

He passed the paper across the table to Karen. She took it and noted the lead officer's name: *Inspector Chris Haws*. She turned to Littleton.

'Can I ask you to make arrangements for Inspector Haws to visit me tomorrow?' She corrected herself as she noticed the time ticking towards 1.45 a.m. 'Sorry, make that later today. I will need time to examine Mr Morrison's body after I get some sleep. Please ask the inspector to come and see me late morning.'

Littleton realized that Dr Laos was now giving him orders. He was too tired to object.

'I'll be sure that he gets the message, Dr Laos.'

'Thank you, Mr Littleton,' she replied. She turned to Dr Rebekah Terrobias.

'And, Dr Terrobias, please meet me at 8 a.m., as I will need your assistance in the mortuary.'

'But I'm only a general practitioner, Dr Laos.'

'That's good enough for me,' said Karen. 'Besides, I will need you to show me the equipment and layout of the mortuary that you have here.'

David Littleton stood up and addressed Rebekah Terrobias.

'Dr Terrobias, please be so kind as to escort Dr Laos to her quarters, will you?'

Terrobias stood up and nodded at her boss. 'Dr Laos,' she said, her attention now on Karen, 'please come with me. We have assigned you your own quarters in a section of the base that is reserved for special guests and civilian personnel. If you need anything, there is a phone next to your bed. Simply dial 112 and the operator will be able to assist you.'

Karen collected her bags and smiled her appreciation. She bid goodnight to the air vice-marshal and followed Dr Terrobias out into the hot night.

When he was sure that Dr Laos and Rebekah Terrobias were out of hearing range, Air Vice-Marshal Littleton walked to the door through which they had departed. He closed and turned a key in the door, ensuring that his office was secure. He returned to his desk and lifted the handset of his office phone. He entered an identity cloaking code and proceeded to dial a local mobile number, with the prefix 99. He listened as the mobile rang. A male voice answered after a few seconds.

'It's me,' said Littleton.

'Why the hell are you calling me at this time of night?' replied the voice at the other end.

'Don't get snappy with me, young man,' Littleton barked back. 'You listen to me and you listen carefully. The Foreign Office have sent a probing, snooty forensic pathologist here and I get the feeling she's going to be asking some awkward questions.'

There was a brief moment of silence as the person on the end of the line thought about how to reply.

'Well, Littleton, you're the boss there, get rid of her.'

'I can't get rid of her,' shouted back Littleton. 'Thanks to your stupidity, this has now gone straight to the fat cats in London and they're hounding me for answers.'

'In that case, Littleton, let them have answers; just keep me out of it. I pay you more than enough money to keep your mouth shut.'

Littleton shifted uncomfortably in his desk chair as the same twang of guilt he had earlier felt now returned.

'The money means nothing,' lied Littleton.

'Oh, is that so?' came the response. Littleton held the receiver away from his ear

73

as if he could somehow separate himself from the mess he knew he had played a part in creating.

'If the money means nothing to you, why don't you return it to us? I'm sure you've been secretly piping it offshore for the last seven years.' The voice laughed and mocked at Littleton.

'What the hell are you talking about, seven years?' David shot back.

'Oh, David, you must be getting senile in your old age. Don't tell me you've forgotten about Beirut?'

Littleton swallowed his pride.

'I put a stop to the Beirut connection years ago,' he said, eager to declare his innocence.

The voice at the other end again laughed. 'I know you did, but it was you that started the Cyprus connection; it seems the taste of dollars is too appealing to you. Planning a nice retirement are we, somewhere peaceful perhaps?'

'So what if I am?' replied David. 'I've earned every penny of that money.'

His words said more than he knew. They told the person at the end of the line that cash was indeed very important to Littleton.

'You'll keep getting your money, Air Vice-Marshal. Just keep your mouth shut and don't tell this pathologist woman any more than she needs to know. If she digs around too much and exposes me, you'll be next on our list.'

Littleton slammed the phone down and wiped the sweat from his forehead. He lifted a folder off his desk and stormed out of his office.

7

Tuesday 21 August, 3.45 a.m.
Colours Nightclub
Ayios Ioannis
Limassol

Sergii Filatov had left Nicosia at 2.30 a.m. and was now parking his black Hummer SUV in the parking lot of Colours Nightclub. He switched the engine off and sat in his vehicle as he drew on the final drags of a cigarette. He looked out of the window and could see the strobe lights on the top floor of the club flashing in time with the beat of the loud club music that vibrated through the building's walls.

Sergii had commandeered control over Colours Nightclub ten years previously, shortly after the then owner, a local by the name of Michalis, had opened the doors for business. Michalis had been unaware that he was opening a nightclub right in the centre of Sergii's turf. He had never heard of Sergii and had been new to the nightclub business. Sergii had attended the opening night, under the guise of being a tourist simply checking out the local nightlife. He had sat for several long hours into the early morning talking to Michalis.

He quickly realized that Michalis was pretty naive and thought a lot of himself. In the space of only three hours, he had told Sergii all that he needed to know: how much rent he was going to pay monthly for the building, how much money his father had bequeathed him upon his death and, more importantly, that Michalis placed so much value on his own arrogance that he had failed to hire security for the club. Sergii had returned the next evening with some heavyweights. He had entered first. His 'boys' — as he called them — had waited outside for thirty minutes before slowly coming in one by one. They had sat at the back of the club's dance floor, out of sight, whilst Sergii had continued to butter up Michalis.

As the night had drawn to a close, Sergii had quietly instructed his biggest heavy-weight, who he liked to call 'Little Sam', to hide inside the club as it closed. Totally oblivious and feeling proud of himself, Michalis had closed the club's doors and was busy counting the night's takings when he had been bundled into a heap on the floor. The keys had been removed from him and Little Sam had tied Michalis like a pig, ready for roasting. Minutes later, Sergii and the rest of his boys had entered. Sergii had played good cop, telling Michalis how much easier and pleasant the experience could be, as Little Sam, in the role of bad cop, had slowly pulled Michalis' right index fingernail loose. Sergii had bent down to floor level and reassured Michalis that there really was no need for such unpleasantness.

Michalis had screamed in pain and finally agreed to Sergii's plans. He would hand over 70 per cent of each night's profits in return for Sergii and his boys working the door as security. Sergii had guaranteed Michalis that he would now be safe. Michalis had little choice other than to accept what Sergii had told him. He once tried to contact the cops but Sergii had already paid them off. They turned a blind eye. As the months had passed, Michalis had become increasingly despondent. His hopes of paying off his sister's mortgage had been dashed and he saw very few options. His previously infectious smile had disappeared from his face, his voice was low in tone and he looked ever more depressed. One night, a year after Sergii had taken over his club, Michalis had failed to arrive for work. Sergii had found him the next morning hanging from a wooden beam in his town apartment. Little Sam had disposed of the body at Kouris Dam, the largest of a network of 107 water dams on the island. At a height of 250 metres above sea level, and sheltered by small villages such as Limnatis and Kryos, it had become a dumping ground for the dead bodies of several individuals that had passed away either directly or indirectly at the hands of Sergii and his boys.

Sergii had used Colours Nightclub ever since that time nine years ago as his preferred base for trading in drugs and narcotics. He had purposefully promoted the club among tourist attractions and had aimed additional marketing material to universities across Europe. As a result, he had managed to establish a small sister company that managed travellers' bookings to the island. Sergii had been pleased with his initiative, persuading young holidaymakers to help finance their trips to the island's resorts by smuggling and dealing initially in Ecstasy, and more recently cocaine and heroin. Sergii's efforts had been made somewhat easier as a result of Cyprus joining the European Union.

Those arriving on the island in possession of a National Identity Card issued by the European Economic Area were not subjected to strict immigration control. A lack of police initiative or sniffer dogs at the island's two busiest airports, Larnaca and Paphos, also meant that drugs were smuggled on average with a 90 per cent success rate. Those that were caught out had ended up in Nicosia's notorious prison. The Turkish Cypriot mafia in the island's north had taken Sergii's lead and successfully managed to use tourists and Turkish citizens travelling via Istanbul to smuggle drugs across the border. The so-called Turkish Republic of Northern Cyprus had inadvertently made their job that much easier: passport holders of the break-away state were recognized only in the eyes of the law by the Turkish government; their travel opportunities other than within Turkey and northern Cyprus were therefore severely restricted and young holidaymakers eager to experience travelling were more willing to get involved with drugs than they would other-wise have been. Their vulnerability lined the greedy pockets of the dealers.

As Sergii appeared at the entrance steps leading down to the club, one of his boys at the door waved to him, telling Sergii that something interesting would be going down inside. He made his way slowly down the flight of stairs and approached his boy who was sitting on a chair at the door's entrance. Sergii had known this employee for five years. He was called Igor. He wasn't the best at his job by anyone's calculation, but was eager to please and Sergii admired his enthusiasm.

'What have you got for me, Igor?' asked Sergii.

'A couple of young lads from the British bases are inside. They claim they were here on Friday night and they want to speak to you. Little Sam's got them in the back room waiting for you.'

'Is that so?' Sergii asked. He pushed past Igor and headed into the club. A few small groups of revellers looked at Sergii as he walked in. He gave them a broad grin and continued past the DJ's box. He pushed his way through a thick black velvet curtain and continued down another flight of stairs. At the bottom of the stairs was a closed door. He took his key and unlocked it. As he walked in he saw Little Sam standing astride two young, lanky boys.

'Well well,' he said as he walked towards them. 'What's going on here, Little Sam?'

Little Sam faced his boss. 'We got ourselves two British soldiers, Sergii.' He sounded pleased with himself.

'Soldiers, Little Sam? They don't look much like soldiers to me. They look more like schoolkids. Is that the best the British have to offer these days?'

He laughed at his own joke. Little Sam copied him. 'Now, what would bring two soldiers here to our good place of work, Little Sam?' asked Sergii, as he made himself comfortable on a chair facing his colleague and the young men.

He looked at the faces of the two young soldiers. Both had been given a few hard slaps. One had a bloody eye and the other a small gash on the right of his neck. Sergii felt impressed by Little Sam's restraint. He had expected by now to see at least a broken arm or two. A bloodied knuckleduster lay on the floor but Sergii saw no sign that it had been used. *It's simply a deterrent*, he told himself. He studied the soldier with the gash to the neck and saw congealed dark blood forming around the wound. He worked out that the soldiers must have been in the club for a few hours already for blood to have begun clotting.

'These kids reckon that you killed a friend of theirs. They say his name was Andrew Morrison. I told them not to make such stupid statements about my boss. They wouldn't listen to me, Sergii. They kept going on and on at me. The drunker they got, the more mouthy they became. They made me give them a beating, honestly they did.'

Sergii comforted his friend. 'Never you mind that, Little Sam. You did the right thing, as you always do.'

Little Sam looked relieved and peered down at the soldiers with his pig face.

'Now step away, Little Sam, and let me talk to these kids.'

Little Sam moved a short distance and positioned himself behind his boss. Sergii moved forwards and reached out as if to help the soldiers to their feet. They stayed where they were on the floor.

'OK, lads, don't stand up, but at least sit like men. It does you no favours, you know; laying down like cowards.'

The boys hesitantly moved into a sitting position.

'There, that's better,' said Sergii, through his teeth. 'Now, why don't we get formally introduced?'

The soldier with the gash on his neck spoke first. 'I'm Danny.'

Sergii waited for more. There was none. 'Is that all you can say: *I'm Danny*?'

'Danny Mills,' the solider replied.

'That's better,' said Sergii.

'And you?' He pointed at the second soldier.

'I'm Phil Wakely.'

The kid had learned it would be better to say his full name, having watched Danny's performance.

'Well, I'm sure you know who I am,' Sergii

replied. 'But, in case you don't, I'm the man you need to speak to. I'm Sergii. What's this Little Sam tells me about you accusing me of killing someone?' He lifted his arms in protest as he spoke, as if to define his innocence.

The two young soldiers looked at one another cautiously.

Phil decided to speak. 'We were here on Friday night and we saw you talking to our mate Andrew. He ended up dead after he left this place.'

Sergii looked shocked. 'Did he? That's a terrible thing to happen to a young man, isn't it?'

Phil appeared confused. Sergii didn't let him speak.

'And what is it that you two do at the British base?' he asked.

Danny answered this time. 'We're new. We're just Officer Cadets looking for some justice for what happened to our mate.'

Sergii nodded. 'And I would do exactly the same if I were you. But let me tell you something about your friend Andrew. Did you know he was a druggie?'

The kids looked shocked.

'Don't talk crap,' said Phil, immediately regretting his words.

It was too late. Sergii had stepped forwards and kicked him directly in the gut.

'That's for swearing at me and calling my good name into disrepute,' he said as he walked back to where he had been standing.

Little Sam looked very pleased with his boss's actions.

'Maybe young Danny would be more willing to talk . . . *politely?*' asked Sergii.

Danny watched his friend gasping for air and decided that it was in his own interest to cooperate.

'I've never heard Andrew talking about drugs.'

'That's very interesting, Danny,' replied Sergii. 'You see, Andrew had quite a taste for the white stuff. Although he hadn't been here on the island very long, he knew where to come to get what he wanted. You know what that means?'

Danny shook his head. Sergii leaned in closer.

'That means that someone told him where to find what he was looking for. You don't have to believe me but I know for sure that your mate Andrew had developed, shall we say, a refined taste. Sadly it wasn't a taste he could afford to keep up.'

'But you said you didn't know Andrew,' Danny said, sure of his memory.

'Now, Danny, don't tell me that little cut on your neck caused you memory loss? I didn't say I didn't know Andrew. I told you I didn't kill him. That's what you accused me of.'

He turned to Little Sam. 'What else did our guests say to you, Little Sam?'

'They told me that unless you told them how Andrew died they were planning to tell their boss at the base about you. They said they would close you down.'

Both Danny and Phil, recalling their earlier alcohol-fuelled courage, looked ashamed. Sergii looked furious.

'Close me down?' he asked menacingly. 'I don't think that's very likely to happen, do you, Little Sam?'

Little Sam chuckled and agreed with his boss that it wasn't very likely at all.

'I tell you what, lads,' said Sergii, drawing on his composure, 'I'm going to give you a choice. Isn't that generous of me?'

Danny and Phil nodded their heads, now anxious to get out of Colours Nightclub.

'Tell me, lads, have you heard of credit versus debit?'

Phil, still in pain both with his eye and from being winded by Sergii, struggled to answer.

'You mean like finances?'

Sergii laughed deeply. 'You could say that. Let's just say that I've just met the two of you in *exactly* the same circumstances in which I met your mate Andrew. He approached me in another of my wonderful establishments, accusing me of murder.' He looked at Little Sam.

'Why is it, Little Sam, that everyone thinks I'm a killer?'

'I don't know, boss. You're the most decent guy I ever met.'

Sergii smirked. 'You hear that, lads? I'm a decent guy. I'll tell you about credit and debit. For everything you do in your life, whether it's personal or related to money or indeed business, every action has two sides: there is a credit and there is a debit. Young Andrew came to me with a blank slate. He told me he had heard that I killed a young soldier called John Riley. Have you heard of Mr Riley?'

Both lads shook their heads.

'Well, I didn't kill Riley. In fact your own bases killed him, indirectly.'

Neither Danny nor Phil believed him, but they had realized it was best to stay quiet.

'When Andrew made such a spurious accusation against my good character, he created a debit. Words don't mean a lot to me, you see, lads. He apologized when he was in exactly the same situation that you two find yourselves in now. I wanted more than an apology. And I got it.'

Sergii looked at both lads. They simply nodded again.

'I told Andrew that he had two choices.' He peered down at Phil and looked him directly in the eyes. He then did the same to Danny before continuing.

'Listen carefully, boys, for those are the same choices I'm about to give you. Either we come to an agreement that I propose in here and the two of you leave, a little worse for wear, but still alive. Or, this room will be the last place you ever see again.'

He studied the fear on the soldiers' faces and knew that he would get what he wanted from them.

'I'm an industrious kind of man. I'm always looking for new staff.'

He looked at Little Sam. 'Isn't that true, Little Sam?'

Little Sam agreed that it was true.

'I can think of nothing better than offering the two of you jobs to work for me. How could you possibly refuse when your life's on the line?'

Danny sighed deeply. 'Tell us what we have to do.'

Little Sam cheered. His boss started clapping.

'That's more what I expect from British

soldiers!' shouted Sergii. 'It's simple, really. You stay here a little while longer and have a small taste of the white powder that Andrew loved so much; for free, of course, as you are my newest employees. Then you go back to the base like nothing ever happened. Give it a day or two and encourage your friends to come here during their down-time. That is how you will earn some credit. After all, it wouldn't be fair to let tonight's small mistake blot your chances of success, would it?'

Danny and Phil both felt terrified. They knew that they had been stupid and overly confident in coming to Colours Nightclub again. The thought that terrified them the most was ending up as Andrew had: murdered. Sergii's tactics had worked. He had gained two new recruits to help him in his plan to tap the British bases and fill them with drugs. He also liked the feeling of power, and the sound of his own voice.

'So, boys,' he continued, 'I'm going to leave you in the capable hands of Little Sam here. He's going to give you something to enjoy; just like Andrew did. I don't want to hear that you have wasted this business opportunity. That's where you can take a different path than that which Andrew ultimately decided to follow — straight to his grave. I expect to see you both here again this coming weekend —

and make sure you bring some friends with you; you really don't want me to be disappointed with you.'

He turned to leave the room, before talking again. 'Oh, and if either of you even think about telling your superiors about what happened here tonight, I'll have you both gutted like fish. Don't forget, if you get tested for drugs back at the base, you're going to be positive for the next few days and you're going to be kicked out the military so quick you won't see it coming. Just think of the shame you'll bring to your families.'

Sergii left the room and locked the door after him, leaving Officer Cadets Mills and Wakely in the hands of Little Sam. As he walked back up the staircase leading to the main floor of the nightclub, Sergii felt proud of his people skills. He had learned the art of manipulation and intimidation. *It works like a charm, every time,* he said under his breath. At the top of the stairs he turned to the bar. He really felt like having a strong whisky.

8

Tuesday 21 August, 7.45 a.m.
Civilian personnel quarters
Episkopi Garrison
Western Sovereign Base Area
Cyprus

Dr Laos had finally fallen asleep at 2.30 a.m. Her bedroom was far from glamorous but it was fully equipped with the basics and necessities: a bed comfortable enough to fall asleep in, a small bathroom joined to her bedroom and, perhaps more importantly, a fully functional air-conditioning unit. Even at this early hour, the sun was already high in the sky and the heat it emitted was extremely strong. Despite having only had four hours of sleep, Karen had woken up and felt refreshed after a long shower and a cup of coffee. It hadn't been her usual choice of blend but she was grateful nonetheless that her room even had a kettle and tea/coffee-making facilities.

Karen knew that she had a full day's work ahead of her. During the night, somebody had slipped an ID badge under her bedroom door that was printed with her name and position, under which the text read *Civilian Contractor*. Not having known whether the base would provide her with work clothes, Karen had packed her own spare set of mortuary gowns. They were at least light and would allow her body to breathe as she worked. She still felt a little taken aback having heard that Rebekah Terrobias, the young regimental medical officer, had not undertaken any kind of examination on Andrew Morrison's corpse. Karen realized that military law was very different from civilian law but had always assumed that some initial post-mortem would be carried out; even to collect blood samples at the very least. Karen had decided this morning to simply do her job as she always did. She had recoiled when she had heard that the previous murder of Second Lieutenant John Riley had simply been brushed under the metaphorical carpet, to better suit political and military needs.

The fact that she had heard this from the air vice-marshal himself left her feeling all the more disturbed. He had told her not to judge the systems and practices that were normal in the military. Karen had decided not to judge: it wasn't her place, she concluded. If that was how this establishment worked, she would simply carry out her work in her professional duties as she had been taught to.

As the clock on her wall moved to exactly 8 a.m., Karen heard a knock at her door. She opened it and saw Dr Rebekah Terrobias standing in front of her, dressed in an identical outfit to that which she was wearing only a few hours earlier. Karen thought that she looked tired and sluggish as she greeted her good morning. They exchanged the usual pleasantries and left together, walking out into the hot sunshine. They crossed a small area of grass and Dr Terrobias led Karen into an adjacent building, with a sign above the entrance that read simply, *S.B.A Medical Facility — Clinical Laboratory*. The room inside was meagre at best. Karen looked around and saw that the very room she was now standing in, which measured about 30 metres in length and 15 in width, was both the clinical laboratory and mortuary.

There was one large refrigerator at the far end, which Karen recognized as a 1970s-issue refrigerator for human remains, known as a conveyor tray system. In the centre of the room stood a pedestal-style autopsy table, which looked to be out of place as it was much more modern than the rest of the furniture and equipment that Karen could see. The autopsy table was one with which Karen was familiar: she had one almost identical back at her own mortuary in Manchester. She recognized the same 100-inch length, 30-inch width and 37-inch height of stainless steel. The table top and large integral sink and grid plates were also stainless steel.

The remaining features were standard issue: a down draft ventilation system, a hydro-aspirator with reversing flow valve, a hose hanger with 8-inch clear PVC tubing. A hot and cold water fixture with a swing spout and vacuum breaker sat under the main stretch of the table itself. Karen felt quite impressed by the table in particular. She certainly hadn't expected to see such a modern design. Karen turned to Rebekah Terrobias.

'Tell me, Rebekah, why has the air vice-marshal assigned you to work with me?'

'It wasn't just the air vice-marshal's idea,' replied Rebekah. 'To be honest, I requested this assignment. He agreed. I always wanted to become a pathologist, but my parents had other ideas; they wanted me to join the military from the age of sixteen. I refused and agreed to join only after I had completed medical training.'

Karen contemplated what she had said. 'Let me guess: your parents are ex-military?'

'Exactly,' said Rebekah.

'Have you ever taken part in an autopsy, Rebekah?' enquired Karen.

'Not exactly; I watched a few during my medical training, but these days most autopsies are closed cases and I have never worked on a real one with a forensic pathologist.'

'Tell me,' said Karen, 'is it true that most medical students now only see autopsies on video demonstrations?'

'Apparently so,' answered Rebekah, 'but I insisted when I was at medical school that they let me see some real ones. It was almost frowned upon for a student to want to see a real autopsy.'

Karen thought it odd, but a lot had changed since she had been a student.

'OK. Well, I won't be asking you for a great deal of help during this procedure. It will be a basic external and internal examination of the victim's body. I will be asking you to assist me with certain aspects, such as ensuring all of the relevant tools are easily accessible. I will also need a Dictaphone as it's good practice to record the entire process from start to finish. Tell me, do you know how to use the table?' She pointed at the pedestal-style autopsy table.

'Actually, I do. Well, I mean, I know the basics. I actually ordered this table.'

Karen was quite taken aback and impressed. 'You did? For what reason?'

'It was six months ago. We used to have a pathologist here; a Dr Steven Higgins, but he was transferred over to the Middle East, where the MOD thought his services would be of more use.'

'Then what did he do here?' asked Karen.

'Not a great deal. He certainly wasn't happy here. He spent almost a year stationed here and never did an autopsy. The air vice-marshal told Dr Higgins that his skills would be better used in the emergency room. Dr Higgins wasn't pleased — understandably — as emergency medicine wasn't his specialty. Other than the occasional chemical dissection of benign tumours and running blood work when soldiers fell sick, he felt that he had wasted a year of his life here.'

'Was Dr Higgins here at the time of the death of John Riley?'

'Yes, he was,' replied Rebekah. 'And he was far from happy when the air vice-marshal told him that there was no need to investigate the soldier's death.'

'That's certainly understandable,' agreed Karen, knowing that she would have strongly objected herself, on moral and professional grounds.

'There wasn't much that Dr Higgins could

do about it in the long run as he was a military officer first and a pathologist second. The air vice-marshal had to remind him of that fact on several occasions. In the end, Dr Higgins decided that he could no longer stay here. He requested an immediate transfer. The air vice-marshal agreed. I assume he is now happily running a mortuary in a combat area over the water.'

'Thank you for the explanation,' said Karen. 'Now, tell me, what made you order the table?'

'I told the air vice-marshal that we might need one in the future. He had persistently refused Dr Higgins' requests, saying that the budgets didn't allow for one. I think he just didn't like Steven Higgins. They never saw eye to eye. I was a little surprised when he agreed to my request.'

'That's understandable,' replied Karen. 'Anyway, I'm glad he did. Now, shall we get started?'

Dr Terrobias went to the far side of the room and changed into sterile, mortuary overalls. By the time she returned, Karen Laos had already positioned the table in a manner that she was comfortable and familiar with. She asked Rebekah to bring Andrew Morrison's body from out of the conveyor tray system. Rebekah wheeled his corpse to where Karen stood waiting. Together, they moved the body onto the table. Karen unzipped the blue body bag in which Andrew had been stored. Rebekah turned on a rather old-fashioned Dictaphone and laid it on a bench nearby, with a small connecting microphone attached to ensure that their voices would be heard.

Karen started, 'This is the recorded entry of an autopsy taking place at S.B.A. Medical Facility — Clinical Laboratory, Episkopi Garrison, Sovereign Base Area, Cyprus. The date is Tuesday August 21st. The time is 8.20 a.m. I confirm that my name is Dr Karen Laos, Consultant Forensic Pathologist. Present too is Dr Rebekah Terrobias, Regimental Medical Officer. The autopsy that will be conducted will examine the body of a young male, identified as Andrew Morrison. I confirm that speculation will not be entertained; only facts as I see them and to the best of my professional opinion will be recorded. Based on scientific evidence further questions for investigation will be recorded accordingly.'

Karen started her external examination. She lifted the victim's head. 'There is a deep indentation, measuring approximately two centimetres in depth and 1.5 in width. Congealed blood around the wound would indicate that the victim was struck by a solid object. The pattern of the injury appears to be consistent with an assault that was unexpected and came from behind. The fact that the victim was found dead in his vehicle would indicate that the victim either trusted his assailant, or the attack was unexpected. Police reports will be able to confirm these suspicions.'

She opened the victim's eyelids. 'The victim's eyes both show signs of pin-prick hemorrhaging of the retinal veins.'

Karen placed her hands around the victim's neck and felt for any unusual markings.

'The victim's neck is bruised and swollen, suggesting further assault with a noose. In general, the victim's body had passed through the entire stage of rigor mortis. The flaccidity of the victim's neck suggests that rigor mortis reached maximum stiffness at approximately twelve hours after death. This would put the timing of complete formation of rigor mortis at 4 p.m. on Saturday August 18th. Time of death would have occurred approximately twelve hours prior to this. With its relatively small diameter, lack of bony shielding, and close association of the airway, spinal cord, and major vessels, the human neck is uniquely vulnerable to life-threatening injuries.'

She then inspected the victim's nasal area. With the use of a small magnifier, she noticed a small hole between the two nasal passages.

'Abnormalities of the victim's nasal area suggest that the victim had used illicit substances.'

She faced Rebekah. 'Dr Terrobias, please take a blood sample and run tests for traces of benzoylmethylecgonine.'

Karen was referring to cocaine. She had seen the same pattern of nasal trauma in many previous autopsies. Dr Terrobias did as requested and stored the blood sample for later investigation.

Karen briefly examined the remainder of the victim's external areas. She saw nothing unusual or suspicious and decided to commence internal examinations. She clicked pause on the Dictaphone and turned to Rebekah Terrobias.

'Rebekah, I am done with my external examinations. It is time for the internal investigation. Are you feeling OK?'

Rebekah nodded. 'Yes, thank you, Dr Laos. I'm really fine with this. I'm learning a great deal from you already.'

Karen reached to the side of the table where she found a standard autopsy knife set. She switched the Dictaphone back onto record mode. She fitted a stainless steel knife with scalpel sharpness into a sterile, easy-to-clean blade holder, which had a safety finger protector and graspable inert plastic handle. With the autopsy knife held in her right hand, Karen cut a large, deep, Y-shaped incision from shoulder to shoulder, meeting at the breastbone and extending all the way down to the victim's pubic bone. She then peeled back surrounding skin, muscle and soft tissue, with the use of a new scalpel. She moved quickly and efficiently with the skill of a professional that had done it a thousand times before. She pulled the chest flap up over the victim's face, exposing the ribcage and neck muscles.

'Preliminary internal examination, both visual and physical, of the victim's neck muscles confirms death by strangulation. It is too early to determine whether strangulation was the primary cause of death.'

Karen made two cuts on either side of the victim's ribcage, and pulled the ribcage from the skeleton. She briefly dissected the tissue behind it in order to check for abnormalities. None were found. She made a further series of cuts to detach the larynx, oesophagus and various arteries and ligaments. She worked quickly and severed the organs' attachment to the spinal cord as well as the attachment to the bladder and rectum. She looked at

Rebekah Terrobias and saw that she had lost some colour in her face.

'Rebekah,' she said. 'Are you still feeling OK?'

'To be honest, Dr Laos, the smell is a bit disturbing.'

'Are you feeling light-headed?' asked Karen as she continued working, pulling out key organs for weighing and further examination. She placed them in sterile containers. Rebekah didn't answer her.

'Go and get some fresh air, Rebekah. That's an order.'

Rebekah quickly left the mortuary and Karen heard the door close behind her. Dr Laos turned to the organs she had removed, and picked up the victim's heart muscle. She placed it on a scale and recorded its weight as 300 grams. She placed it back into the container from which she had taken it. She then removed the liver and kidneys, and weighed them. The liver weighed in at 1,500 grams. Karen recorded it as an average weight for a male of Andrew's age.

'The victim's liver is of normal dimensions and weight. However, there is evidence of some fatty liver, suggesting damage by alcohol. Damage may also have been caused by benzoylmethylecgonine. Blood work will reveal such results in due course.'

Rebekah Terrobias walked back into the examination room, looking more like herself. Karen smiled at her as she walked in. Karen proceeded to open the victim's stomach, to check its contents. She had learned long ago that in most autopsies, the contents of the stomach are an important piece of evidence, which can sometimes prove to be the difference between accidental death and foul play.

She recalled her old lecturer at medical school telling her: *'We have all seen the television and cinema autopsies played out where the pathologist will empty the contents of the deceased's stomach and will analyze them with a view to establishing what they ate and when they ate it; this despite what you might think is not the stuff of media legend and is actually a very useful tool in the pathologist's arsenal.'*

These were words that Dr Laos had never forgotten. She emptied the contents of Andrew Morrison's stomach and spoke as she worked, mostly for the benefit of Rebekah Terrobias.

'The process through which food is absorbed into the body can take anything from twenty-two hours to two days to complete and within that time food is broken down and reduced to a liquid pulp from which essential proteins are extracted. The victim's stomach contents in this case indicate that he digested pizza, probably in a period of two hours leading up to his death. Pizza takes approximately two hours to digest; the process of digestion was interrupted by the victim's murder.'

She took a sample of liquid from the stomach contents and turned to Rebekah.

'Dr Terrobias, please have this sample analyzed. If the deceased had been using illicit substances, traces will also be present in the stomach juices.'

Rebekah Terrobias dutifully took the sample from Dr Laos. Just as Dr Laos was finishing with the investigation of the stomach, she stopped suddenly.

'Dr Terrobias, what do you make of this?' She had seen something that she had almost missed.

Rebekah approached the table. 'That's a small bag, Dr Laos,' she said, a look of confusion on her face.

'Indeed, Dr Terrobias. I have seen this before, not often but I would make an educated guess from what I have seen of the victim's body so far that the contents of that bag will be found to contain cocaine.'

Karen paused the record mode on the Dictaphone.

'Dr Terrobias,' she said, 'do you know what time Inspector Haws is coming?'

'I would expect it will be late morning, as you asked for,' replied Rebekah.

Karen had forgotten that she had purposefully asked for late morning as she knew she would need a few hours to complete the autopsy of Andrew Morrison.

'Of course, thank you.'

She was deep in thought.

'There is only one known reason for ingesting cocaine,' Karen said. 'That is for the purposes of smuggling. Of course, it is for the police to determine, but I am beginning to suspect that Andrew Morrison was smuggling cocaine into the base.'

Rebekah looked shocked and troubled. She remained silent.

Karen looked at Andrew's body and pushed from her mind the question that she most wanted to know the answer to, '*What were you doing, Andrew?*' She knew that she had to complete the autopsy. Although she already had some ideas about cause of death going around in her mind, having seen the head injury and strangulation marks, Karen Laos knew that she would be negligent were she not to continue searching and checking for signs of further trauma. She restarted the Dictaphone once more.

'At this stage of the autopsy process, I will remove the victim's brain and confirm any further signs of trauma, and attempt to verify the evidence found on the exterior of the victim's body.'

Dr Laos proceeded to remove the body block from the back. She placed it behind the victim's neck like a pillow, raising the patient's head to make it easier to remove the brain within. She took a clean scalpel and made a large incision from behind one ear, across the forehead, to the other ear and back around. She then divided the cut and pulled the scalp away from the skull in two flaps. She placed the front flap over the victim's face and the rear flap over the back of the neck. She asked Dr Terrobias to pass her an electric saw. With this she started to cut and created a cap, which she then pried off, exposing the brain. With the cap pulled off, the soft tissue membrane that covers the brain remained attached to the bottom of the skull cap. With the brain now exposed, Karen proceeded to sever the brain's connection to the spinal cord and tentorium, a thin membrane that connected and covered the cerebellum and occipital lobes of the cerebrum, and lifted the victim's brain from out of its skull. She examined it for several minutes.

'The victim's brain is of normal size and

weight. However, there are signs of internal bleeding. The pattern of the haemorrhage spreads out in an outward direction towards the victim's inner ears. Visual inspection further indicates damage to the rear of the victim's brain. The occipital lobe at the back of the cerebral cortex has impact marks, consistent with those found on visual examination on the back of the victim's head at the start of this autopsy.'

She looked over at Rebekah Terrobias.

'Dr Terrobias, what can you tell me about injury to the occipital lobe?'

Rebekah contemplated her answer. 'The victim would have experienced severe disorientation and confusion. Injury to the occipital lobe would also account for the haemorrhage you described.'

'Correct,' replied Karen, aware that she sounded like a lecturer. She walked around the autopsy table and spoke aloud.

'The time is now 10.15 a.m. My impression is that the victim, Andrew Morrison, died from a primary cause of a blunt head injury, which caused massive internal injury. Secondary cause of death is strangulation. The victim also appears to have used illicit substances, as evidenced by liver injury, nasal damage and of course the finding of concealed cocaine in the victim's stomach.

There is no evidence to suggest that the victim was force-fed the drugs. I would surmise that he took them willingly, of his own volition. Blood work will be run for confirmation of cocaine abuse and results will be included in my final report.'

Karen turned off the Dictaphone and turned back to Dr Terrobias.

'Rebekah,' she said, 'we now have a duty of care towards Andrew's remains. His body is open and the chest cavity is empty with butterflied chest flaps; the top of the skull is missing and the skull flaps are pulled over the face and neck. What do you suggest we do now?' Karen was testing her younger colleague's knowledge.

Rebekah stepped forwards. 'I assume that other than the victim's liver, the bag of cocaine and the stomach fluids, which we need to retain for further testing, we will either incinerate the remaining organs or place them back into the victim's body.'

'Yes,' replied Karen. 'That is standard procedure. I would suggest incineration of the victim's organs that are not required. Please collect them for disposal.'

Rebekah did as Dr Laos had asked. Karen took a five-minute break before finalizing the autopsy. She started by closing the chest flaps and then delicately sewed them back together. She then moved to place the skull cap back in its place and, whilst Rebekah held it in position, she closed and sewed the scalp.

'Andrew's body is now ready for repatriation,' Karen said as she signed an official release form. 'Please let me know when the blood work is available, Rebekah. I am going to go back to my quarters and start typing the autopsy report.'

Rebekah stayed to sterilize the mortuary and clean the equipment. Although she had learnt a great deal from Dr Laos, she wouldn't say that she had particularly enjoyed the experience.

9

Tuesday 21 August, 11.00 a.m.
Office of Inspector Chris Haws
Sovereign Base Areas Police Headquarters
Episkopi Garrison
Western Sovereign Base Area
Cyprus

Inspector Haws was a tall man of almost six feet. Aged forty-three years now, he had been based in Episkopi in the Western Sovereign Base Areas for four years. Inspector Haws had trained as a soldier when he was just sixteen years of age. The military had been a part of his family for more than half his life. His wife, Patricia, was a nurse by training but had in the last two years not worked. Chris and Patricia Haws had been delighted two years previously to announce the birth of their first child, Dillon, a lively, happy child. Chris, Patricia and Dillon lived in a charming semi-detached house, situated on the top of a large cliff that overlooked the peninsula. The street they lived on was appropriately named Isle of Wight Street; a characteristic English name based upon an actual UK location shared by all the base-owned properties.

Chris Haws took the lead strategic command over the Criminal Investigations Division of the Western Sovereign Base Area's Military Police Division. Chris Haws upheld military law efficiently and patrolled both Akrotiri and Episkopi bases in his troop car. He also regularly patrolled outlying areas and villages. The population over which he held investigative command numbered approximately 14,000 people; including around 7,000 native Cypriots whose houses fell within the territory of the bases' administration. The remaining number of individuals were made up by the British military and their families. Given the approximate 50-50 split of British and Cypriot residents that lived and worked on the bases, either as military personnel or civilian contractors, Chris Haws was careful to be seen to work closely and actively with his colleagues from the Republic of Cyprus Joint Police Unit. His counterpart, a Mr Dimitris Andreou, was considered a seasoned professional, fluent in both Greek and English, the official languages of the British bases, and respected by both populations in equal regard.

Although based permanently in Limassol's divisional police headquarters, Andreou split his time — and his duties — fairly and evenly between the base and his office in Limassol. He had been given a small office of his own on the bases, close to the office of Inspector Haws. Chris Haws knew when to call on the assistance of his colleague. It had been the first thing he had done early on Saturday morning when the lifeless body of Andrew Morrison had been discovered by a local farmer tending his land. The farmer had called the general emergency number for the island, but because of his location when he found the body, his call had been diverted to the switchboard of the British bases. Inspector Haws had been off-duty at home and had been awoken by an early-morning call from one of his junior officers.

Chris Haws had been immediately affected by the murder of one of the soldiers that he so carefully tried to protect. He had accompanied a small team from his office to the scene of the crime, and some paramedical personnel. Dr Rebekah Terrobias had been the only qualified medical practitioner present, there simply to sign the death certificate to confirm Morrison's death. It had been a relatively short journey for Inspector Haws, taking him only ten minutes to arrive at the scene. He didn't know Andrew Morrison personally but, as with all the soldiers, recognized his face immediately.

Inspector Haws had wanted justice on the first murder case in which Second Lieutenant John Riley had died. He had refrained from pushing his superiors, including Air Vice-Marshal Littleton, to be allowed to do his job as a cop as he understood that it was a case that had already been shut down by powers far higher up than he. His position was somewhat difficult at the best of times. Haws liked to think of himself as a cop first and soldier second.

It was an ambition that he had struggled with immensely. Several issues reminded him that, in fact, he was a soldier first. His uniform was very different to that worn by 'normal' cops. The car he drove was decorated differently. He carried a gun at all times; his non-military police colleagues back home in the UK did not. Where their priority sat with protecting the laws handed down by the elected British Parliament, Chris Haw's priorities were dictated by the Ministry of Defence, an unelected body that had full jurisdiction over the laws that they imposed. When they had decided, therefore, that John Riley's death would not be fully investigated, Inspector Haws had had to fall in line and comply.

He had asked Dimitris Andreou to keep hush about the most recent murder and had informed Andreou that it looked this time as if the MOD were pulling out all the stops to investigate the death properly this time around. He had heard that they had even drafted in the help of a civilian forensic pathologist. The inspector was anxious to meet Dr Karen Laos. He checked his time and saw that it might be acceptable now to visit Dr Laos. She had asked for a late-morning meeting and this was pretty late-morning. He collected his keys and kitbag and headed out to his car.

Tuesday 21 August, 11.35 a.m.
Civilian personnel quarters
Episkopi Garrison
Western Sovereign Base Area
Cyprus

Karen Laos had quickly typed the findings from the autopsy of Andrew Morrison. Standard procedure dictated that she succinctly summarize the autopsy examination itself, leading to the culmination of the generation of the final autopsy report. Karen had realized early into her career that each report, although sharing similar basic qualities, always had its own unique flavour, depending on whether the autopsy had been

114

relatively simple and straightforward or voluminous and exceedingly complex.

As a general rule of thumb, autopsies conducted on murder victims were always more complex than those carried out on, for example, individuals that had died by natural causes. Karen scanned through the report that she had just finished writing, checking to ensure that it contained a description of her findings and that it assembled and correlated these findings with the clinical setting and laboratory results — which she was still waiting for.

She made a note stating that the report was still pending blood-work analysis. Other than that, Karen was quite satisfied with her findings. The report was the product of the post-mortem anatomic examination, as well as constituting a complete assessment and integration of the victim's clinical data, brought together to provide a purposeful accounting of the information and facts. She stood up from the small desk on which she had typed the report on her laptop, and yawned.

Karen always felt tired after working an autopsy; she had concluded long ago that the tiredness was her body's way of dissipating tension and stress.

A sharp knock on her door told Karen that

she had a guest. She opened the door and found herself facing Inspector Chris Haws.

'Dr Laos?' he asked, with a Geordie accent, undiminished by his time overseas.

'Yes, I assume that you are Inspector Haws?' replied Karen.

They shook hands.

'Inspector, I have just this minute finished the autopsy report following my investigation on Mr Morrison's body. I'm afraid I have no access to a printer to give you a hard copy, but perhaps we can head somewhere and have a chat?'

'Slow down, Dr Laos,' laughed the inspector. 'I'm not here to grill you. I just came to introduce myself. But yes, it would be a very good idea for us to go elsewhere. There is a great staff canteen just a five-minute walk from here. How does that sound to you?'

'Superb,' Karen replied as she collected her laptop and placed it back in its protective bag.

As they left the room, Inspector Haws turned to Karen.

'I don't want to be presumptuous, Doctor, but did you find anything definitive in the autopsy on Lieutenant Morrison?'

Karen looked at him. 'Yes Inspector. Let's just say that one could say Andrew Morrison was both a victim and a perpetrator.'

The inspector looked confused. 'How do you mean?' he asked.

'That, Inspector, is going to be your job to discover. I can tell you that Andrew was murdered. Now, I don't know why he was murdered, but it seems that he had secrets. I'm sure that the use of illicit drugs is forbidden on all military bases?'

'Of course, Dr Laos; why do you ask?'

'Well, Inspector, Andrew had concealed cocaine in a small bag in his stomach, which would lead me to believe that either he was an occasional, personal user, or he was smuggling it in to sell. As I said before, that will be your job to discover. I will of course help you as much as I can. Let's go and sit down in the canteen, Inspector. There is no point standing here in the corridor.'

'Of course, Dr Laos, I'm sorry, I wasn't being nosy. I just want to get to the bottom of this case as soon as possible. What you have just told me, however, makes the whole thing seem more complicated than it was before. As if a murder isn't bad enough.'

Karen sensed that this was a cop that had gotten a little too used to the quiet life in the sun.

'Maybe your autopsy report will clarify things for me,' he added.

'Inspector,' said Karen, 'the value of the autopsy, no matter how thorough and skilfully performed, is greatly diminished if the findings and correlations cannot be adequately communicated to end users of the information. I'll tell you more when we are sitting down.'

Tuesday 21 August, 12.10 p.m.
Zygi Taverna
Aphrodite Hills Resort
Paphos District
Cyprus

Charlie Charalambos and his partner, Rafaela, a woman in her mid-twenties of Greek-Cypriot descent, sat underneath a large, shaded pergola adorned by an ancient grapevine at Zygi's Taverna. The taverna was situated on the outskirts of the Paphos district, set high above the ocean with unobstructed views of the Mediterranean which, at this time of the year, glistened a turquoise blue. The region, Aphrodite Hills, had been so named due to the legend that here, in the oceans beneath Zygi's Taverna, the goddess of love and beauty, Aphrodite, had been born of sea foam. The region had seen immense development in recent years with an international eighteen-hole golf course spanning the length of the main beach road. A five-star hotel had also been built, sharing the same name of the goddess.

Although the owners of the taverna had not been bothered by Charlie over the years, they were wary of him, given his reputation. They remained polite but slightly aloof whenever he visited. Charlie of course gave the impression that they were his best friends, showering them with unwanted gifts and praise every time he entered the premises. He spoke loudly this lunchtime and gave his partner little room to talk or contribute to the conversation. They had been joined by Rafaela's best friend, Nikoleta, and her boyfriend. They too were in their twenties.

Charlie had long ago sworn Rafaela to secrecy with regard to how he made his money. She often wondered therefore, as she did today, why he spoke so loudly and openly bragged about his 'business' in front of the general public. Charlie had the unconscious habit of switching rapidly between the Greek and English languages. The average Cypriot could follow his conversation to a point; English tourists on the other hand found themselves unable to concentrate on their own conversations, with Charlie's incessant chatter elevated to a high volume.

'I like to think of myself as a people's person,' said Charlie to Rafaela's friends. 'I'm always available to lend a listening ear. Isn't that right, sweetheart?' he said to Rafaela, placing his hand on her right leg.

She simply nodded, knowing the futility of even attempting to change the conversation to something not related to Charlie.

'Any time you need me,' he continued, sipping on a pint of local Keo beer, 'you just let me know and I'll sort things out.' His eyes moved like darts across the table, watching his companion's reactions.

'What is it that you do?' asked Rafaela's best friend.

'A bit of this, a bit of that; not all legal if you catch my drift,' he replied, a small laugh laced into his words.

Rafaela noticed a small group of tourists seated about eight metres to their right side. One of the men had looked up in Charlie's direction as he spoke, but Charlie had been oblivious to it.

'Speak in Greek, Charlie,' interrupted Rafaela, indicating the presence of eavesdroppers.

'No need for that, love,' he replied. 'We're all friends here.' He took a deep gulp of his beer before continuing, 'I'm in business with a Russian at the moment, you know. He's a big guy, thinks he knows it all, but he does what he's told.'

Here he goes again, Rafaela thought, *pretending like he's the boss of the universe.* Rafaela had met Sergii and suspected that it was really he that controlled her boyfriend's so-called business empire. She wouldn't ever tell Charlie that he was a weak imitation of Sergii, but she certainly thought it enough. Sergii seemed like a man who had brains and thought carefully about his movements; Charlie on the other hand had managed to ingratiate himself to important people through fear and — she had to admit — a certain type of flair for convincing people that he knew best. Somehow, she accepted, his methods worked. *Through either sheer luck or persistence.*

She knew that he had his demons; she knew too that he was a troubled soul and had told herself that she would be his saviour one day.

'And what is it that you do with the Russian?' pressed Rafaela's friend.

'Let's just say we make a lot of money by seeing opportunities for business where most people don't.' Charlie felt pleased with himself and his answer. Rafaela's friend wasn't willing to let the subject rest, unaware that she could be treading on dangerous ground.

'What kind of opportunities?'

Rafaela shot her a look that told her to change the topic.

'I only ask Charlie because it's so hard to find work these days.'

Good tactic, girlfriend, Rafaela told herself.

'If it's work you're looking for, why didn't you just say so in the first place?' asked Charlie. 'I'm sure I can hook you up with something that will bring you in some cash.'

Rafaela secretly took her phone from her bag and sent her friend a message, saying simply, *refuse.* Fortunately, her friend had her mobile on silent, vibrate mode. She immediately saw the secret text.

'I'll keep it in mind. Thanks, Charlie,' she replied.

Charlie lifted his hand and called the waiter over. 'Another Keo, please, and whatever my friends are having.'

He flashed a wad of cash, making sure that Rafaela's friends would see it. Nikoleta's boyfriend simply nodded his appreciation. He had a feeling that Charlie was not someone he wanted to spend much time with. It certainly explained his silence.

'Yep,' continued Charlie, commanding the group's attention further, 'we certainly know how to make money. As my mum always said,

God rest her soul, money makes the world go round. Just this week I've pocketed more money than you'd make in a lifetime.'

Rafaela felt embarrassed: not just for herself but for her friends.

'The secret of making money is in knowing how to beat your competition. And when your competition steps up the pace, you either do the same or you take them down.'

He laughed loudly. 'Take the British bases, for example. I'm no fan, but being a Londoner myself, I understand why they cling onto their small patch of land here in Cyprus. They make money and they do it pretty damn well. Not as well as I do,' he added, 'but I've got some good friends there and they know a business opportunity when they see one. I'm not just talking about insignificant friends; these are folk that have positions of power. And with power comes money.'

'Let's not bore Nikoleta with all this business talk, Charlie,' said Rafaela, aware that her boyfriend was again letting his ego rule his behaviour.

'OK, love,' he replied. 'I'm just oiling the wheels of conversation. And what a beautiful day it is for it, too.'

He looked up at the blue, cloudless sky, keen to impress his girlfriend's mates. 'Ah, yes, life is good. You have to stay one step ahead at all times, Nikoleta, that's the trick. I'll give you an example. One young lad from the British bases this week thought that he could outsmart me. You know what happened to him?'

Nikoleta shook her head.

'Let's just say he won't be doing anything like that ever again.' He laughed again, louder than previously. Stimulated by alcohol and with an ego to match, Charlie had failed to notice an old nemesis from Paphos sitting alone on a table just out of sight from where Charlie, Rafaela and her friends were having their drinks. Detective Andreas Ioannou had known Charlie for many years. Charlie had tried to buy this cop's silence and cooperation but Andreas had not been persuaded by Charlie's money or fazed by his notoriety.

He knew that several of his colleagues had been bought out by Charlie Charalambos, but Detective Ioannou had been determined to find a way to bring down Charlie and his little empire for too many years to give in. He had followed Charlie whenever the opportunity had arisen. He had learnt much this lunchtime, all of which he had been recording on his mobile phone. He had a feeling he knew who the *big Russian* was that he had heard Charlie talking about, but couldn't be sure. He quietly stood up and walked away from the taverna from a side exit hidden by tall eucalyptus trees. He spent a minute mentally ticking off a list of Limassol cops he knew to be decent. In order to find out what the hell Charlie Charalambos was up to at the British bases, he knew he would need the help of his colleagues in Limassol.

He clicked his fingers together with excitement as he remembered Inspector Dimitris Andreou who worked with the Cyprus Joint Police Unit at the British bases. He walked to his car and got in. He scanned through his mobile phone and came to Andreou's number. He hit 'call' and waited for the inspector to answer.

10

Karen sat at an orange and black plastic-backed seat and table, waiting for Inspector Haws to return from the counter of the canteen, where he was buying two coffees. Karen had instructed him that hers must be filter coffee, no sugar, and extra milk. He had said that he preferred espresso. Dr Laos always associated espresso with a trip she had made to Paris. Despite her best efforts, she had been unable to find anywhere that sold what she called a *normal coffee*. Every coffee shop and bar that she had been to had served her the strong espresso that she had a particular dislike for. She always needed a large glass of water to wash the taste away.

Inspector Haws had tried to convince Karen to have the same as him, on the grounds that when he first moved to Cyprus

126

he had also had no fondness for the stronger shots of coffee, but that with time he had developed an appreciation for it. The thought of drinking that thick, syrupy drink caused Karen to feel some discomfort. She opened her laptop and found the autopsy file that she had only a little over an hour ago finished writing.

'So, Dr Laos,' said the inspector as he returned to the table. 'Tell me more about the cocaine you say you found in Andrew Morrison's body.'

'There's not much to say at this stage,' she replied, studying the screen in front of her. 'I found the concealed bag of cocaine in Mr Morrison's stomach during the autopsy. It was wrapped, as is frequently the case in those that ingest drugs for the purposes of smuggling, in a strong plastic material, which would have been impervious to the body's digestion process. Had Mr Morrison not died as a result of murder, he was running quite a risk transporting drugs in such a fashion. There are often times when those that smuggle narcotics in this way die as a result of a rupture of the plastic in which the drugs are wrapped; the contents seep out uncontrolled into the circulatory system and cause systemic failure leading to death.'

'That sounds particularly unpleasant,' the inspector said.

'Indeed,' Karen agreed. 'I've asked Dr Terrobias to run a definitive test on the contents found in Mr Morrison's stomach. However, it is almost certain that pathological examination will confirm my suspicions that the content is indeed cocaine. Further evidence for this assumption comes from both interior and external examination during the autopsy process. Mr Morrison's nasal passages showed clear signs of cocaine use; small but detectable holes and damage in the nasal passage lining, again evidence of cocaine use. Further to this, my investigations revealed that his liver had started to show signs of interior damage; small amounts of what we call fatty liver are perfectly normal in those that abuse alcohol, for example, but given Mr Morrison's age, and the additional liver damage I detected by way of physical scar tissue, I cannot conclude that alcohol alone was the cause.'

Inspector Haws looked troubled.

'Dr Laos,' he said, 'the idea that one of our own soldiers was murdered is bleak enough, but if your investigations conclude that the victim was a user of illegal substances and had been smuggling them into the base, we are faced with an entirely more complex and difficult scenario.'

'I think I know where this is heading,' replied Dr Laos. 'You are quite rightly concerned that Andrew Morrison may not have been alone in his use of cocaine and fearful that other soldiers on the base may be involved.'

'That is exactly what I am concerned about,' confirmed the inspector. 'I also have no other choice than to treat Mr Morrison's murder as all the more suspicious than it is already. Although we never had the opportunity to conduct an autopsy on John Riley's body when he was killed, the manner in which he was found and the circumstances of his demise are very similar to the current circumstances we find ourselves presented with by Lieutenant Morrison's death. Excuse me for one minute, will you please, Dr Laos? I need to ask Air Vice-Marshal Littleton to join us.'

The inspector pulled his mobile phone from his shirt and called the air vice-marshal. He spoke briefly and hung up.

'He will be with us in the next few moments, Dr Laos,' he confirmed.

'I agree that the air vice-marshal needs to be involved,' said Karen. 'But what is it exactly that you are thinking?' She could see by Inspector Haws' facial expression that there was something else on his already troubled mind.

'Did you know that we have in the region of 7,000 personnel spread across the bases at any one time?'

'I didn't know the exact number,' said Karen. 'But I did do my research before I came here. I realized that the population of the bases stands at around 14,000 people.'

'That's true,' replied the inspector. 'But half of that number is accounted for by the local, native population that lives on and farms the areas that fall under our jurisdiction.'

Karen performed a quick mental calculation. 'I assume that you're not telling me this in order to give me a lesson on the local population census?' she asked.

'No, I'm not, Dr Laos. I'm telling you the numbers to give you an idea of the kind of scale we are faced with if we were to recommence drug screenings.'

Before Dr Laos had the chance to answer, the air vice-marshal entered the canteen, looking red in the face and sweaty from the heat. For his benefit, Dr Laos repeated the findings from her autopsy to David Littleton.

'Oh my God,' he said, seemingly shocked. 'That's awful news, Dr Laos.'

His eyes twitched nervously between Karen and Chris Haws.

'How long will it be before you can definitively confirm your findings from the autopsy?'

'Mr Littleton,' said Karen, 'the blood work from Dr Terrobias will be only a formality confirming what I have already said. What's important now is to concentrate on how this problem can be tackled.'

'I agree,' piped in Inspector Haws.

'Wait a second both of you, please,' said the air vice-marshal. 'I refuse to believe that my base is a breeding ground for drug smugglers and I have no intention of allowing the two of you to turn it into a hostile or antagonistic centre of interrogation.'

Dr Laos sensed that her earlier suspicions about the air vice-marshal being less than professional were about to come true.

'I understand your resistance, Mr Littleton, but I would have thought you would be the first person who would want this case solved in a timely and skilled manner. The opportunity is being presented to you here and now and I really don't understand why you seemingly want this problem to be brushed away — as, if I may add, was apparently done after the death of John Riley.'

Inspector Haws saw the air vice-marshal's

face grow redder and decided to step in. He looked at Littleton.

'Sir, I was just explaining to Dr Laos as you arrived that we have in the region of 7,000 personnel on the bases and to drug-screen them all would be virtually impossible.'

Littleton jumped in as he saw his chance.

'That's quite right, Inspector, it would be impossible. More to the point it would create a climate of fear among our soldiers and their families.' He looked smug with himself.

'That's odd,' said Karen. 'I would have thought that allowing drug smuggling and potentially more murders on the base would create more of a climate of fear.'

The air vice-marshal appeared ruffled as Karen continued to speak.

'I am by no means a military person, but I would have thought that drug-testing would be routine, as it is in other professions, such as nursing, medicine, social care and even for seafarers. Why isn't it implemented here?'

'That was my decision,' explained Littleton. 'After I arrived here seven years ago I decided, with the power that is invested in me, to stop all compulsory drug screens here on the bases. It was a costly and unnecessary procedure that wasted thousands of pounds' worth of time and money every month.'

'More costly than murder?' asked Karen.

'That's unfair, Dr Laos,' replied the air vice-marshal through grated teeth.

Inspector Haws again interrupted. 'Sir, with your permission I am going to reimplement random drug screens for all personnel currently on the base. Of course we can't test the local Cypriot population as that would be a violation of their human rights, but we are perfectly within our rights to investigate this murder with the use of any methods we see fit; and that includes testing all military personnel.'

'And what if I don't approve of this intervention?' asked the air vice-marshal under his breath.

'Well, sir, that would be a most unfortunate situation to be faced with. But if you did refuse I would simply go straight to the Ministry of Defence in London as well as the Military Court of the Sovereign Base Area asking for this intervention to be enforced.'

Karen thought that the growing tension in the room could have been cut with a knife, so tense it was becoming.

'Very well,' said Littleton. 'Since my opinion as the commanding officer no longer seems to carry any weight, I will authorize your little plan. But I want it known that this is being done against my better judgment. I also want it stated for the record that I will not allow, or authorize, enforced drug screens on civilian personnel that work here on the bases.'

'Thank you, sir,' said Inspector Haws sarcastically. He turned to Karen. 'Dr Laos, as soon as the funding approval comes through, which I expect will be in the next several hours, I will need to ask for your continued help in implementing the procedure.'

'It would be my pleasure,' replied Karen.

Littleton stood up. 'I think I'm done here. Keep me updated will you?'

He didn't wait for an answer and stormed out of the canteen. A few soldiers sitting at the far end of the room averted their gaze as he walked past. They hadn't heard the conversation but they had certainly picked up on the fact that a heated exchange had just taken place between the air vice-marshal and the inspector. Word had spread quickly about the arrival of a forensic pathologist and the death of Andrew Morrison. One of the soldiers looked at Karen and assumed that she was the civilian pathologist in question.

'I think we got our point across,' said Karen. 'I find it very unusual that the commanding officer is so averse to our plan.'

Inspector Haws looked at Karen and

lowered his voice. 'To be honest with you, Dr Laos, I am not that surprised. I have known Littleton for four years and I have never had much faith in him.'

'Why do you say that?' Karen asked curiously.

'For a number of reasons, Dr Laos, the least of all being my own intuition. The air vice-marshal has repeatedly blocked my attempts in other investigations ever since I arrived here four years ago. I thought at first that it was simply his unique and quirky style of management, which isn't that unusual with the older generation of soldiers. But I soon realized that Littleton projects a caring front, on the basis of what I think is a pretence of maintaining a close-knit family under his command. As you have just seen, he doesn't like to be questioned and is easily agitated when pulled up on his decision-making process. You handled yourself well.'

Karen smiled at him. 'I only said what I believe as a professional. I don't need him to like me, Inspector; simply to allow me to do the job I am being paid for. Otherwise, there is no reason for me to be here in the first place.'

'Well,' replied the inspector, 'I for one am glad you're here.'

'Thank you, Inspector. Now tell me, is the

trade in illicit drugs a big problem here on the island?'

The inspector collected his thoughts. 'Actually, yes it is. My understanding is that it's a problem that is growing. My colleagues in the Cypriot police tell me that until the late 1980s the issue of drugs wasn't one that affected the island.'

'What happened in the late 1980s?' Karen asked.

'A massive influx of Russian and Eastern European mafia. Add to that, UK-based criminal gangs organizing and profiting from drug-backed holiday campaigns and the market was quickly saturated with narcotics. The local police here thought they had erased the problem: until Ayia Napa.'

'The clubbing resort?' Karen enquired.

'Yes, to the north-east of Larnaca. The early 1990s saw a boom in the number of young clubbers choosing Cyprus as their preferred destination to Ibiza. The so-called mob resurfaced and took advantage of the youngsters. There was a time, so I am told, that traditional Cypriot family ties and law and order came close to collapsing as a result of the drugs trade. You know, there used to be a time here on the island that people would leave their houses unlocked and not have to worry about someone breaking in and

136

stealing their possessions. That aspect of the culture has all but vanished.'

'What did the police do about it?' Karen asked.

'They started imprisoning and fining any tourist found to be in possession of, or dealing in, illicit substances.'

'And how did the *mob* respond?'

'They got clever, and became more elusive. Some say they paid off the local cops and cut them a share of the proceeds. I know that's possible on an island this small. But I also know some excellent local cops. I work with my counterpart, Inspector Dimitris Andreou of the Cyprus Joint Police Unit, very closely. He is aware of the murder on Saturday morning. He is trying his best to keep it hushed outside the base for now but if we are to stand any chance of rooting out the cause of the problems, I know that we can rely on his help.'

'In that case,' Karen said, 'I look forward to meeting him.'

'You will do, sooner rather than later I expect,' replied Chris Haws. 'Until that time, what do you say to our visiting Dr Rebekah Terrobias to see whether she has the blood results you're waiting for?'

Karen checked her watch: 1.30 p.m.

'If she has the same pathology facilities

available to her here that I have back home, the results should be ready by now. I get the feeling that Rebekah has been thrown in the deep end here.'

'In that case, she is lucky to have your help, Dr Laos,' said the inspector.

Karen collected her laptop and packed it away.

As they walked out, Inspector Haws paused. 'I don't want to overstep my mark, Dr Laos. But your surname; it's quite common here. Are you Cypriot by any chance?'

Karen laughed. 'Does my thick Manchester accent sound very Cypriot?' she teased.

'No, but your name is definitely Greek. You wouldn't have seen it yet, as you've only been on the base since you arrived. But if and when you venture out, you will see your name on the roof of most houses.'

Karen looked perplexed. 'What do you mean?'

'The water tanks, Dr Laos. Most houses have water tanks on the roof, and most of those water tanks have your surname on them.'

Karen suppressed a giggle. 'So, I'm related to a water tank, inspector?' she joked.

'No!' he laughed. 'But there's a family here on the island called Laos that have a massive investment in construction and building.'

'Well,' Karen replied, more thoughtfully. 'My paternal grandfather was Greek-Cypriot, that's where my name comes from. But I don't know any of my living relatives in Cyprus. I know that they exist but I don't know who or where they are.'

'In that case,' said the inspector, 'I'm sure that Dimitris Andreou will be able to help you find your family, if of course you're looking for them.'

'Since I'm here already, it might be interesting to find them,' she replied.

'Inspector Andreou will be more than happy to help you. Not only in finding your family but also in solving this case. He will be impressed by your connection to the island.'

They turned and left the canteen.

★ ★ ★

Air Vice-Marshal Littleton lifted the phone on his desk and, using the same identity cloaking code he had used so many times now, called his contact with the local 99 mobile phone prefix.

'What do you want, Littleton?' The voice had answered his call immediately. 'I'm trying to get some sleep here.'

'Sleep?' barked the air vice-marshal. 'The

damn pathologist has made friends with the inspector that heads up the military police here. She's also done her autopsy on Andrew Morrison. You idiot! You gave him the cocaine to carry and then had him killed?' he asked.

'He accepted the cocaine before he left on Friday night. He was killed after he changed his mind. Keep your head low. Is this why you're calling me and waking me up?'

'No, not only. The damn cop threatened me with the Ministry of Defence unless I agreed to reimplementing the drug-screening policy.'

'Did you agree?'

'Of course I did. I have to be seen to be cooperating.' The sweat dripped down Littleton's face and he felt his heartbeat increase.

'Well, I hope you made it clear to the cop that you wouldn't be agreeing to civilian employees being obliged to take drug screens?'

'I'm not that stupid,' replied Littleton. 'They will be testing the soldiers randomly.'

'That's not ideal,' the voice replied. 'Still, it's better they're not testing the other staff. We need to protect Stanislav.'

'I know that. That's exactly why I refused to let them test the civilians. But you know they can push the matter if they want to.'

'Then don't let them. That's what I pay

you for, to keep things running as smoothly as I tell you to.'

'There's going to be more deaths out of this. I can tell,' Littleton snarled.

'It's called collateral damage. You know that as well as anyone. Keep your cool and stop bloody well calling me. The last thing I need is you panicking.'

Littleton's contact ended the call, leaving the air vice-marshal alone with this thoughts. He felt, for the first time, as uneasy as he had back in Beirut before he had arrived in Cyprus. He knew that he had made a monumental error in judgment for the second time in his career.

He wished now that he had refused to have any part in his contact's plans. He wished too that he had better and more wisely used his posting to Cyprus as a chance to create a clean slate for his prior wrongdoings. Subconsciously he knew that it was too late for that. Time moved in strange ways and affected all that it encountered in its own style and was the ultimate nemesis that the air vice-marshal had no control over.

11

Tuesday 21 August, 2 p.m.
Office of the inspector
Divisional Police Headquarters
Limassol
Cyprus

Inspector Dimitris Andreou had not spoken to his old colleague, Detective Andreas Ioannou from Paphos, for a long time. They had seen one another in passing over recent years as the government attempted to crack down on police corruption by transferring officers between towns in an attempt to cut out nepotism. The local population had been complaining that officers that only worked in their home towns were increasingly refusing to fine or ticket their non-police friends and family members. The discrepancy had led to police officers being transferred at weekends to other units and divisions.

Inspector Andreou was acutely aware of the problems on the island that had come about as a result of the drugs trade. He also knew of Charlie Charalambos, and of the reputation that he had created and perfected over the years. Charalambos had long been on the police radar, but they had never been able to get a firm grip on his criminality, not least of all because he had so successfully managed to pay off bent cops. The information that Detective Ioannou had given him therefore seemed too good to be true. A murder on the British bases timed so perfectly with Charalambos boasting in public about a lad from the British bases? OK, reasoned Andreou, he hadn't confessed to a crime but he had certainly insinuated knowledge about one; that may be good enough as a start. He had also suggested that he was directly related to the young soldier's demise. Andreou knew that there was a missing link in the puzzle that was unfolding. He had to figure out what that was. Who was the Russian that Charlie had boasted of working with? Was it the equally elusive and slippery Sergii Filatov? Andreou had stopped counting the number of opportunities he had lost over the years to snare Filatov. Filatov had terrorized Limassol for two decades. His quick thinking and fast cash meant that the police had been unable to ever pin anything firm on him or his associates. They had many leads and suggestions with regard to Sergii's actions but a complete lack of facts to support them. Potential witnesses over the years had either mysteriously vanished or changed their mind at the last minute when it came to giving evidence against Filatov.

Any chance to connect Charlie Charalambos with Sergii Filatov would be too tempting to simply ignore. Inspector Andreou racked his brain trying to think of how and why Filatov and/or Charalambos would be involved with the murder at the British bases. He drew a blank in exasperation. The circumstantial evidence spoke volumes; he knew a great deal about both Filatov and Charalambos and knew they were both equally capable of enacting high-level involvement in the murder on the bases. He also knew that both had amassed their respective wealth through dealing in drugs. But they were clever; they always had an alibi — always managed to evade conviction. It was something they had been doing for years. They were therefore experts in their game. If Andreou were to raise his own chances of finally putting an end to their legacy of crime, he knew that he had to try to think more like them.

Knowing that the two were opportunistic feeders told Andreou that neither of them would hesitate to move quickly when they saw an opportunity to make money. *Think like a piece of greedy filth*, Andreou urged himself. *What is it that drives Filatov and Charalambos? What makes them do what they do? Money? Certainly. Reputation?* They both had that in abundance already. Would they really do something that threatened their safety? They were impulsive. Andreou therefore concluded, as he had for many years, that one or both of them would one day fall foul of their own smugness and arrogance. He hoped that day was getting closer.

He decided it was time for Inspector Chris Haws to pay him back the favour he had done him by keeping quiet about the murder at the bases. He hadn't pursued the matter himself as the inspector held overall command of the sovereign base area where the body had been found. But the fact that a local had found the body meant that Andreou had the right to get involved. He had an obligation to get involved, all the more so given what he had heard from Detective Ioannou. He also had a level of privilege that came by virtue of his work with the Cyprus Joint Police Unit. With this in mind, he headed for his car and made the twenty-five-minute trip to Episkopi Garrison.

Tuesday 21 August, 2.10 p.m.
S.B.A Medical Facility — Clinical Labora-
   tory
Episkopi Garrison
Western Sovereign Base Area
Cyprus

Dr Rebekah Terrobias had felt excited and slightly proud of herself. The fact that she had been given some temporary respite from dealing with routine medical cases since Dr Karen Laos had arrived made her re-examine her professional role. She was grateful for the opportunities that the military had given her; the chance to serve her country overseas, the ability to travel the world: these were things she certainly did not take for granted. But the thrill of working with Dr Laos on a murder investigation was something quite unique. She secretly wondered whether she would be happy going back to her normal duties; stitching up wounded soldiers or bandaging the occasional broken ankle.

Her time in Cyprus had been relatively peaceful. She wasn't exactly in a war zone. Had she been posted a little further afield, another couple of hours to the east, she would be on the borders of Afghanistan and working perhaps in a medical camp in the middle of a combat zone. There, she knew, she would have more than the basic duties of a general practitioner to fulfil. Was it too late to take further professional training to become a fully registered forensic pathologist? She wasn't sure. Would she able to deal daily with dead bodies and cut them up in the precise and efficient way that Dr Laos had this morning? Rebekah Terrobias thought that with further experience she would be able to do the job just fine.

She had just finished running the tests that Dr Laos had asked for as Inspector Haws and Karen Laos entered the laboratory. Rebekah beamed a wide smile as the two entered.

'Do we have any results yet, Rebekah?' asked Karen. 'The inspector and I are keen to move forwards with our investigations.'

'Good news, Dr Laos,' replied Rebekah. 'Your suspicions were correct about the contents of the plastic bag found in Lieutenant Andrew Morrison's stomach. I have sampled the substance and can confirm that it is benzoylmethylecgonine.'

'That,' said Karen, looking at the inspector, 'is cocaine.'

'Thanks for the explanation; just how technical is this going to get?'

'That depends,' Karen replied, 'on the kind of facilities that Dr Terrobias has had at her disposal. There are several ways to determine the composition, quality and indeed origins of various drugs, including cocaine. Older-style investigative techniques are less accurate than those that are commonly used these days.'

Dr Terrobias spoke up. 'Well, I am pleased to say that I located a little-used piece of equipment that I am sure you, Dr Laos, are more than familiar with. It is the SNIF-NMR system.'

Karen looked impressed. 'You have SNIF here?'

The inspector looked perplexed. 'What is SNIF-NMR?' he asked, quite predictably. Karen wanted to give Rebekah Terrobias the chance to explain it. She gestured to the young doctor to continue.

'SNIF-NMR stands for site-specific isotopic fractionation by deuterium NMR. It quite simply allows us to detect the unique synthetic deuterium sites of the drug as well as, in the case of cocaine, a further fifteen natural deuterium-labelled sites. The natural properties of the drug have the potential to tell us the geographic location of the original source of the drug; whereas the synthetic sites assist in developing a workable theory about the commercial sources that could be used to convert the coca leaf into cocaine.'

'Well said, Rebekah.' Karen smiled at a

clearly pleased Dr Terrobias. She turned to Inspector Haws. 'What do you know about cocaine, Inspector?' she asked.

'Other than the fact that it's an illegal Class A drug that causes massive financial, health and personal pain, not a great deal.'

'You forgot something,' replied Dr Laos. 'It is an extremely sought-after and valuable drug among drug-traffickers. The fact that it is linked to the murder of a soldier on this base is not something that any of us should lose sight of. Most of the cocaine that is smuggled around the world originates, in its purest form, of course, in South America; specifically in Colombia, Ecuador, Peru and Bolivia; areas which are all rich in the coca leaf. If we look at the bigger picture here, being able to determine the origin of illicit substances can assist massively in international intelligence operations. Dr Terrobias, please continue.'

Terrobias lifted a printed report. 'The sample found in Mr Morrison's stomach originates from a highly refined source, suggesting, as Dr Laos said moments ago, that the cocaine he ingested was of an extremely high financial value. Therefore, those that gave him the substance would need to have recourse to potentially vast sums of money.'

Inspector Haws made a note of this fact. He knew that it would help in his investigation. If he could locate dealers on the island with such large financial resources, he would be able to determine who were likely suspects and those that he could exclude.

'Older methodologies that predate the technology afforded to us by SNIF-NMR relied on identifying specific processing impurities and minor alkaloids present in illicitly produced cocaine. Given the fact that we have a highly refined, much purer sample of the drug, SNIF-NMR is the most efficient technology available to us. It is also a popular piece of technology that has been widely used to determine the geographic origin, adulteration and authenticity of many natural products, such as wine, tobacco and fruit juices. SNIF-NMR is also a patented, universally accepted approach in forensic science investigations.'

Dr Terrobias paused briefly. 'I am not a forensic scientist, unlike Dr Laos, but I must say that SNIF-NMR is also very user-friendly. The model of SNIF we have is a Bruker AM-500 NMR, which is equipped with a 10mm broadband probe, and operates at 76MHz for deuterium, with proton decoupling and a fluorine-19 lock. The sample of cocaine was prepared and accomplished with the use of a Walter's 991 photodiode array detector.'

The door to the laboratory swung open unexpectedly and Inspector Dimitris Andreou walked in, taking the wind slightly out of Dr Terrobias' sails. He immediately greeted Inspector Chris Haws; somewhat like an old friend, Karen noted.

'I'm sorry to barge in on you all,' he said with an excellent command of the English language.

'I was somehow expecting that you would show up sooner or later,' replied Chris Haws. 'Let me introduce you to my colleagues.' He gestured towards Karen. 'This is Dr Laos, the consultant forensic pathologist I told you about.'

'Very pleased to meet you,' said Andreou, shaking Karen's hand and adding, 'A fellow islander, I believe.'

Karen gave him a look that affirmed his statement, but remained silent.

Inspector Haws continued. 'I believe you may know Dr Terrobias? She is our resident regimental medical officer. She has been, quite impressively, assisting Dr Laos with her autopsy and findings on the body of Lieutenant Andrew Morrison. She has also been explaining the results of the findings from Dr Laos' autopsy.'

'In that case, it seems that I have arrived at

just the right time.'

'You will be interested to know that Mr Morrison had apparently been smuggling cocaine into the bases; Dr Laos found a small, concealed bag of the drug in the victim's stomach,' said Inspector Haws.

Dimitris Andreou gave a look that gave away a thousand thoughts in one glance. 'That is very interesting. It also may well link quite nicely to what I have to tell you. That, however, can wait for now. I'd quite like to hear what Dr Terrobias is saying. If you don't mind, of course?'

Dr Laos nodded as Rebekah delivered her conclusions. The inspector, unfamiliar with the technical jargon, decided to sit down and wait until he felt he had something to say.

'I then applied a freeze-drying technique to the sample, with an Alcatel-model high-vacuum pump. This allowed me to detect benzoylmethylecgonine and related alkaloids. The sample found in Mr Morrison's stomach was of a purity of 97 per cent of the drug's base compound.'

'I understand that is extremely high?' queried Inspector Haws.

Karen intervened. 'Indeed it is, Inspector. I expect that Dr Terrobias will be able to tell us now from where the drug originated.'

She looked at Rebekah Terrobias for

confirmation. Rebekah felt that she was being cut short in her deliberation. She was enjoying talking the technical talk and felt that she had impressed Dr Laos. She had certainly impressed herself somewhat. Nevertheless, she understood that the inspector really only wanted to hear aspects that would assist him in his investigation.

'That's correct, Dr Laos. The benzoylmethylecgonine can be traced definitively to a South American location. I would surmise there is a 98.6 per cent probability that the specific drug found in Mr Morrison originated in Peru. I did some subjective Google searches whilst I was waiting for the test results of the cocaine to come back. The test results show that the level of purity inherent in the benzoylmethylecgonine could only have been achieved locally in Peru. The drug gangs there use a specific technique of cultivation that places a kind of DNA trace on the drug's origin. My less-than-scientific findings from Google tell me that the drug producers stamp their own mark in order to keep rival gangs from staking a claim in one another's production. I also learnt that coca cultivation is surging once again in Peru's remote tropical valleys, part of a major repositioning of the Andean drug trade that is making Peru a contender to surpass

Colombia as the world's largest exporter of cocaine. The traffickers — fortified by the resilient demand for cocaine in the United States, Brazil and parts of Europe — are stymieing efforts to combat the drug's resurgence in the country and are raising the spectre of greater violence in a nation still haunted by years of war.'

'What does that mean, generally, for the global fight against drug traffickers?' asked Inspector Haws, feeling now that the conversation was more in line with a topic he could contribute to.

Karen Laos was more than happy to leave her younger and now more enthusiastic colleague to continue.

'That's a good question, Inspector.' She spent a few seconds contemplating her response. She had read a great deal.

'The increase in Peru offers a window into one of the most vexing aspects of the American-financed war against drugs in Latin America, which began in earnest four decades ago. When anti-narcotics forces succeed in one place — as they recently have in Colombia, which has received more than $5 billion in American aid this decade — cultivation shifts to other corners of the Andes. More recently, coca growers moved to dozens of new areas within Colombia after aerial spraying in other areas. Scholars of the Andean drug war call this the *balloon effect*, bringing to mind a balloon that swells in one spot when another is squeezed. Washington's policy of supply-oriented intervention inevitably improves the efficiencies and entrepreneurial skills of traffickers. The balloon effect — and its consequences — seem to be coming full circle in the jungle valleys of central Peru, the cocaine industry's storied cradle. By the 1970s, with cocaine illegal and Peru's government outlawing much of the new coca cultivation in the country, Colombian drug lords put in motion another boom, exporting Peruvian coca leaf to cocaine laboratories across the border. Columns of the Shining Path later worked to protect farmers growing coca in the region, consolidating Peru as the world's top coca grower. In the 1990s, President Alberto Fujimori militarized the region to crush the Shining Path, lowering cultivation levels. Now many farmers are planting coca once again. Some even claim that coca lets them feed their children, due to its high cultivation yield.

'The increased cultivation in central Peru contrasts with the situation in Colombia, where cultivation fell 18 per cent in 2008, according to the United Nations. In Peru, cultivation climbed 4.5 per cent that year, capping a decade in which areas under cultivation had increased 45 per cent since 1998. Cultivation is also rising in Bolivia, though that country remains third in overall production.'

Dr Laos interrupted her young colleague. 'So we have established that there is indeed a multinational and apparently highly profitable trade in cocaine. Now, my question comes back to Mr Morrison and how such a trade may be infiltrating Cyprus as a whole and, more generally, the British bases.'

She looked at Dr Terrobias. 'But thank you, Rebekah, your work is very much appreciated; you have been very insightful. I assume that analysis from the victim's stomach liquids also confirms that he had used cocaine, prior to his death?'

'Yes, it does, Dr Laos. Not only was Andrew smuggling drugs into the base, pathology results from the contents of his stomach and analysis of his blood confirm that Mr Morrison did indeed have a personal habit. Further to that, the physical scarring that you found on his liver during the autopsy confirms that the lieutenant had been using the drug for quite some time.'

12

Tuesday 21 August, 3.15 p.m.
S.B.A Medical Facility — Clinical Labora-
tory
Episkopi Garrison
Western Sovereign Base Area
Cyprus

Inspector Andreou stepped forward.

'There are a number of dealers on the island that are well known to the local police. However, there are only a small handful that I would say have the potential access to the kind of money required to deal with cocaine of the quality that you found in Mr Morrison's stomach.' He looked thoughtfully at Inspector Haws. 'Chris, would you agree that this is now a case that we can work on together? I ask because I have a couple of leads that we could follow up more quickly together, rather than if we were to work alone. The leads I have in mind would require our collaboration. I have two potential suspects that may well lead us to the source of the drug problem and potentially to the individual — or individuals — that killed

157

Lieutenant Morrison. Given that both of the suspects I have in mind are residents of the Republic of Cyprus, they do not strictly fall under your jurisdiction. However, if we were able to link them to the recent crime, you would have an obligation to get involved.'

Inspector Haws raised his eyebrows. 'You have suspects already?' he asked his friend.

'*Potential* suspects,' replied Andreou. 'A colleague of mine in Paphos overheard a well-known gangster by the name of Charlie Charalambos talking, as he does always — loudly and verbosely — commanding the attention of everyone around him. It's sometimes difficult with Charlie to know whether he is talking about events that are true or something entirely fictional; I get the impression he isn't completely well psychologically. However, on this occasion he was heard saying that he has recently been making money with the help of a Russian, whose name he didn't say. I have some ideas about who that Russian might be; but more on that later. Suffice it to say, Charalambos implied directly — and on record I may add, as my colleague recorded the entire conversation covertly — that he had had close involvement with, and I quote from my colleague's recording now: '*one young lad from the*

British bases *this week who thought that he could outsmart me. You know what happened to him? Let's just say he won't be doing anything like that ever again.'* He also said that he had *'powerful friends'* here on the bases.'

'Impressive,' said Dr Laos. 'I'm not a cop but I have worked closely in my profession with cops over the years, some better than others. What you just said sounds to me like you have enough initial suspicion to bring this Charlie guy in.'

Andreou looked hesitant. 'I'm afraid it won't be that easy, Dr Laos. Charlie Charalambos is two things: a vile gangster but also a very powerful man. I'm afraid that we need something much more concrete to go on before we even touch Charalambos. However, I have already asked some of my undercover guys to track him over the next few days. I want to know who the Russian is that he was talking about. I have a suspicion that his name will turn out to be Sergii Filatov; another nasty piece of work that has terrorized the island for far too long. He is also the same as Charlie Charalambos in that he is very powerful; he too has amassed his wealth through the use of intimidation and fear. He differs from Charalambos in one important aspect.'

'What's that?' asked Inspector Haws.

'He would never sit in public and brag about his activities.'

'It doesn't sound like this Filatov will be as easy to finger as Charalambos,' Karen said.

'Maybe not,' replied Andreou. 'However, we've lost too many opportunities already to get a grasp on these two characters over the years. I for one don't want to miss what may be the best chance we have. Although we can't directly arrest them, we can watch them. I have been on their tail for a long time; longer than I care to recall, as has my colleague, Detective Ioannou in Paphos. Something tells me that they will ultimately be the cause of their own downfall.'

Dr Laos had been thinking about something else that Inspector Andreou had said. She saw her moment to speak.

'Inspector, you also said that Charlie Charalambos suggested he had *powerful friends* here on the base?'

'Yes, Dr Laos, but something tells me that may have been something Charalambos said to exaggerate his position and importance; believe me, he does that all the time.'

'I certainly do believe you, Inspector. I'm just saying that perhaps we shouldn't be so quick to dismiss this out of hand.'

160

'I agree,' interjected Inspector Haws, much to Karen's relief. 'I expect that once we start the drug-screening agenda more leads will ultimately come to light by themselves.'

He turned to Andreou. 'And, if your suspicion is correct about Filatov and Charalambos one day being the cause of their own downfall, then let's give them an opportunity to take that fall.'

Karen addressed Inspector Andreou, 'Didn't you say that Charalambos is somewhat psychologically disturbed?'

'For sure he is. Years of drugs and violence have warped his brain; of that there can be no doubt,' the inspector said with certainty.

'Well, I wouldn't usually suggest this, but why don't you take advantage of that fact and bring his psychological demons to the surface? With the use of your undercover cops following him, maybe he will break.'

'That does sound pretty inhumane, Dr Laos,' answered Inspector Haws. 'But possibly effective. What do you think?' he asked Andreou.

'Let's see. The undercover guys will start tracking him today and report back to me. If Charlie spots them, he will certainly feel rattled. When he gets rattled he usually reacts violently, which means another opportunity to get to him may present itself to us.'

Tuesday 21 August, 4 p.m.
Officer Cadets' Barrack; Block B6
Episkopi Garrison
Western Sovereign Base Area
Cyprus

Although it was unusual for officer cadets to be assigned overseas experience so early into their training with the military, it was not unheard of. Episkopi Garrison, under the auspices of Air Vice-Marshal David Littleton, had been more than willing to welcome young future officers for on-the-job work experience. Littleton had certainly seen the lucrative potential in that strategic move. Officer Cadets Danny Mills and Phil Wakely had both been afforded the opportunity to spend August and September of this year in Cyprus. Young and keen to travel and learn, they had both jumped at the chance. The lottery system that selected cadets for overseas assignment had been kind to them. Now into their third week on the base, both young cadets were wishing that the system hadn't been quite so 'kind' in its selection of their names.

Danny Mills had been stationed previously for his training at a military base in Staines, which had put him close to where his parents lived in Twickenham. Phil Wakely had also been close to his own family at a military base in Norfolk. Although they had only known one another for a few weeks, the two had developed a close friendship. They had been given shared accommodation in Block B of the designated Officer Cadets' Barrack at Episkopi Garrison. Their shared room was basic in every way: two single beds were positioned at opposite sides of the room from one another. A faded blue square-cut carpet covered the floor. A sink for shared use had been shoddily plumbed into the room. One wardrobe for shared use sat practically in front of the only window in the bedroom, meaning that natural daylight had been totally obscured.

No air conditioning had been installed in this barrack; a ceiling fan that was operated by a pull-string had been the only source of moving air that the two young soldiers had been given. Not that it had made much difference in the middle of August. Their sleep, therefore, had been poor since they had arrived at the base. It had not, however, until now been as poor as this morning. They had finally been released from Colours Night-club's 'basement' by Little Sam at 6.30 a.m., feeling initially as if the world were one big rollercoaster ride to be enjoyed.

Little Sam had encouraged the reluctant

lads to have a smoke on his love-rose 'straight shooter'. He had explained to them that smoking cocaine was his preferred method but that with time they would, as Andrew had, develop their own preferences for ingesting the drug. Afraid of not only the drug itself but the price that Sergii had told them that they would pay for not complying, both Danny and Phil had decided it would be best to get it over and done with. Little Sam had been keen and willing to show the young soldiers how to smoke cocaine. He had shown them where to place a small piece of clean heavy copper, which would serve as a reduction base and flow modulator in which the 'rock' was subsequently melted and boiled to vapour.

They had inhaled the fumes, nervously at first, until Little Sam had forced their heads into position. The effects had been immediate gratification and a sense of joy that neither had previously experienced. Five minutes later, the first wave of the thrill had worn off. The boys wanted more and to be released to go home. Little Sam had thought that they needed to try more of the rock, or *my little diamond*, as he had called it. He had given them another hour of pleasure before telling them to *fuck off and get out* at 6.30 a.m.

They had driven back to the base along the

same back roads that Andrew Morrison had taken. Little Sam had told them that they wouldn't be spotted and that he would arrange for someone to meet them at the entrance to the base. They hadn't spoken a great deal on their return journey. Danny had driven as Phil had looked spaced-out and distant. He had also been emotional, breaking down in tears, and had seemed paranoid. Danny had told him that things would get better and that the way he was feeling was perfectly normal after taking cocaine. Although not feeling too great himself, Danny had decided to pretend to Phil that he knew what he was talking about. *Get a good sleep, mate*, he had told him on the journey back to the bases. *We'll find a way out of this mess.* He didn't believe his own words and knew for damn sure that Phil didn't, if he had even heard him.

Following Little Sam's advice, Danny had driven the old road and followed a sign that would take them back into the base via the civilian personnel's checkpoint. There, a gateman neither of them had ever seen before, calling himself Stanislav, had greeted them and told them to follow his car. He had escorted them through the bases in an area that was unfamiliar. He delivered them close to their barrack and had driven away, after telling them that he would be seeing them again soon.

Phil had passed out within a few minutes of getting into his bed, still fully dressed in the same clothes that he had worn the previous night. Danny, feeling in more of a contemplative state, had sat on his bed thinking about what had happened and, more importantly, what he could do to get out of ever having to go back to Colours Nightclub. He didn't want to fuck up his career just as it was beginning and felt protective of Phil, who he had never seen in such a state. Ever since leaving Colours Nightclub, he had seemed increasingly concerned with his own perception of 'being guilty'. Danny hoped that when Phil woke up, he would be feeling better.

Danny finally fell asleep at 8.30 a.m. and woke up slightly confused and thirsty after seven hours. As he got out of his bed, he looked around and noticed that Phil wasn't in his bed; he couldn't see him anywhere in the room. He checked the time and felt alarmed that he hadn't woken up earlier. He thought that he remembered a dream but quickly realized it had been the sound of Phil crying a few hours earlier. As he remembered the early morning at the club and Phil's reaction afterwards, he jumped up from the side of his bed and went to the sink to get a glass of water.

He splashed his face and filled the glass. He took a long sip. It was then as he studied his tired face in the mirror that time seemed to slow down. In one dreadful second he saw the lifeless body of Phil Wakely hanging in the wardrobe, the darkened room making his reflection in the mirror all the more ghostly. That one instant of time seemed to last for ever. In that short second, Danny Mills experienced the full range of emotions from shock to panic and fear and others in between that he couldn't name. The sound of his glass smashing in the sink below made him move. He tried not to look in the mirror and felt an immense pressure building against his spine, an unusual and physical sensation of shock. Acting on instinct and an impulsive need to get the hell out of the room where Phil's dead body now lay half-suspended and visible through the crack of the wardrobe door, Officer Cadet Mills fled from the bedroom, slamming the door shut after him.

He reached the corridor outside, felt dizzy and steadied himself, his hands against the wall. He could hear the sound of soldiers outside busily engaged in training exercises. The sun came strong and bright through the windows of the corridor, momentarily blinding him. He waited until the colour spots had left his eyes and hurried down the staircase that led to the ground floor.

What the fuck am I going to do? Should I go back? Check that he is really dead? What if I tell someone? But who? I know! That guy Stanislav. How will I explain what happened? No, that won't work. Shit, shit, shit. I'm going to be killed if I talk to him. He must know that creep Little Sam and his boss Sergii. How else would he have known to expect us this morning? I've got to get the hell away from here. Anywhere. Just away from this fucked-up mess.

He found the exit at the bottom of the stairs. He moved more cautiously now, not wanting to be seen by the soldiers training outside. He opened the door slowly and exited into the thick heat, becoming aware for the first time since his awful shock that he was wearing only a pair of shorts, a T-shirt and flip-flops. He had no clue as to where to go. He took some deep breaths and tried to think rationally. He contemplated going straight to the air vice-marshal. He dismissed that idea as useless, terrified of the trouble he would get into. A military court at the very least. *If I run, where am I going to run to, dressed like this? I've got no money with me.*

I don't even have my phone. He tried to consider his options but every name that came to his head, the air vice-marshal, the gateman, Stanislav, Inspector Chris Haws, the local cops, all drew an equally unpleasant conclusion.

Having decided to act on his gut feeling and without plan or purpose, he headed along the same track that he had driven several hours earlier, well concealed from sight. He reached the end and watched two guards at the civilian entrance talking to one another. He couldn't see any sign of Stanislav. *Better,* he told himself. He took off his flip-flops and held them in his hand. He moved quietly past the back of the guards' building and tucked himself in behind a length of eucalyptus and followed it until he saw a small dirt road and fields and the Mediterranean Sea in the distance. Checking that there were no signs of traffic, Danny Mills ran as fast as he could into the brown and scorched fields that spanned out ahead of him.

13

Tuesday 21 August, 9 p.m.
No 34, Domnitsas Street
Kallepia
Paphos
Cyprus

'Will you stop pacing around, please? I'm trying to watch some television,' Rafaela pleaded to her boyfriend Charlie, who had been on edge ever since he arrived home an hour earlier.

'They're after me this time. I know it. I feel it in my bones and all my senses tell me they're watching me.'

He continued to pace backwards and forwards along the length of the marble-floored living room. Charlie was moving more briskly than usual, his wiry body hop-scotching now towards the sideboard where he kept his favourite alcohol. He leaned down and opened the door, taking a bottle of Absolut Vanilla Vodka. He poured himself a large shot, added an inch of lemonade and walked back across the room to the windows. He peered through the curtain.

'Who is watching you, Charlie?' asked Rafaela.

'I don't know. Someone, anyone. Make a list,' he replied, clearly irritated.

Rafaela decided to try to calm her boyfriend down.

'Listen, darling, you've had a long day. I'm not saying you're wrong but even if someone is watching you, you've been in these situations before. Just ignore them and pretend they're not there.'

She hadn't seen any signs of their house being watched but made the decision to humour Charlie's convictions. She had realized a long time ago that when Charlie was in one of these moods, it was the best thing to do. His mood changed so frequently and rapidly that she found it difficult to keep up with him. In the morning he had been sullen and grumpy. By lunchtime he was talking so much she couldn't get a word in edgewise and now he was angry and agitated.

There was a distance in his eyes that told her he was getting close to snapping. She had dealt with his rapidly changing moods for long enough to see and recognize that same familiar glassy look. He turned back from the window.

'I was out doing my work, checking on my businesses when I first saw them. It was just after your friends left from lunch. How well do you know them?'

Rafaela knew where this was heading. Charlie trusted only a very few people at the best of times; a trust that was always strained and liable to break. She stood up from the sofa and walked towards him.

'Charlie, I've known Nikoleta for years, ever since I was a little girl. You've met her before, several times, you just don't remember because you're so preoccupied.'

'Are you calling me stupid?' he snapped back at her.

'No, I'm not. I'm just saying I know how busy you are and when you're busy you tend to forget people that you don't see day in, day out.'

He sighed deeply. 'You're probably right. I am very busy. I'm only so busy 'cos I'm trying to keep us in the good life.'

He reached towards Rafaela and lifted her cheek, a little harder than usual.

'I know how much it means to you,' he said, his hand firmly cupping her chin.

She thought that he might lean in to kiss her but instead he dropped her cheek and walked back to the window.

'Two men,' he said, his voice muffled from behind the curtains. 'I saw two strange men following me. I'm sure of it.'

'And what did they look like?' asked Rafaela, sure now that she wasn't going to be able to get any rest this evening.

'Quiet, nasty-looking men,' he exaggerated. 'Cypriot, definitely. Smartly dressed, dark hair, one of them about 175cm, with dark shades, about thirty-four years old. His mate was smaller, fatter, a bit of a porker and older.'

'You paid *that* much attention to them?'

'I pay attention to everyone. I have to. It's what keeps me — and you — safe. I first saw them when I stopped at a kiosk to buy some smokes after I left the tavern. The fatty was in the queue behind me. He sweated a lot. I saw him again an hour later when I was up in Tsada village checking on that souvenir shop I took over last year.'

Charlie spoke as if he were reading from a pre-written list. 'He was sitting in a dark car. I didn't think fast enough, or I would have gone and asked him why he was following me.'

'And how about the taller one?' Rafaela asked. 'When did you see him?'

Charlie felt as if his suspicions were confirmed because his girlfriend apparently believed him. 'He was far more elusive; much smarter than the porker.'

He walked back to the sideboard, and

poured himself another drink. He spoke loudly as he returned. 'The tall guy stayed out of sight after I spotted him outside the kiosk where his fat friend was inside. I didn't see him at Tsada.'

He threw his arms in the air. 'They saw me come home!' he shouted, his voice growing louder once more.

Rafaela stepped towards the window too. 'What do you mean, they saw you come home?' She sounded more genuinely accepting of Charlie's story than she had initially. She looked through the curtain and didn't give him the chance to reply. 'Charlie, our house is hidden by that massive wall and you've got CCTV cameras on every corner. No one can get in or out without us knowing about it.'

'It was as I pulled into the driveway. I remember it exactly now. I was on my mobile to Sergii and the daylight was fading. I opened the car window to aim the key fob at the electric gates so I could get in. I looked in the wing mirrors as I always do and I saw the car again. They clocked me looking at them and started to drive off.'

'Well then, Charlie, keep your cool. They're gone for now. Just check tomorrow to make sure they're not following you. If they are, give them a wave, don't let them rile you like this; it's not good for your health,' Rafaela said, sensibly. The last thing she wanted was to lose the life to which she had grown accustomed.

'And what if they are out to get me?'

'You'll know soon enough,' replied Rafaela, now stroking Charlie's chest. 'You always do. If it comes to it, do what you do best; beat them to the mark. If they're new boys in town looking to bring you down, bring them down first.'

She winked at him.

'You're a good girl, Rafaela. What would I do without you?'

That was exactly what Rafaela wanted to hear. Though quiet most of the time, she knew when to speak up. She did it well. Charlie didn't see the extent to which she manipulated him. But then, he was a manipulator of the highest degree. They suited one another nicely.

14

Air Vice-Marshal Littleton had managed, quite well, to avoid contact with Major General Morrison and his wife since they had arrived on the base in the early hours of Tuesday morning. The major general had left a number of messages with Littleton's secretary requesting an appointment to discuss his son's death. Littleton had purposefully deflected the issue for as long as he could. He knew that it would be a difficult meeting but the retired major general was well aware that the autopsy on his son had been completed and was now actively seeking answers.

Littleton had arrived at his desk early this morning. His secretary had called him shortly after his arrival, giving him his usual morning handover of the events on the base. All seemed peaceful enough, other than the fact

176

that the major general had again been calling. Littleton had told his secretary that he would see the major general today. *The earlier the better*, he had thought. *Put on a front, say how sorry you are and get the old man out of your hair*. Littleton didn't like himself for thinking like this, but knew that he had a lot going on right now. He had a copy of Dr Laos' autopsy report on his desk and was already prepping himself about how he would deliver the findings. He also wondered how he would manage to stare an old colleague and friend in the face and explain the drugs connection. *Put on an act, Littleton; that's what you've been doing all these years anyway, isn't it?* The same shard of guilt stabbed deep in his stomach. His secretary called and informed him that the major general and his wife were waiting for him.

'Send them in,' he replied grimly.

His office door opened and the major general entered, two steps ahead of his wife. 'Please, come in,' said Littleton, standing up and walking around his desk. He took the major general's hand and put on his best guilt-free and empathetic look.

'I'm so sorry and so devastated at your terrible loss, Graham,' he said, calling the major general by his first name. He turned to Graham's wife. 'And Suzanne, I can't imagine what you're going through. Please, both of you sit down. Can I get you anything at all?'

'No, David, we're fine,' Graham replied. 'We just want to find out what happened to Andrew and get back to the UK to give him a decent burial, that's all.'

'Of course you do. I understand completely,' Littleton lied. 'Well, I do have a copy of Andrew's autopsy report. I can assure you both,' he continued, looking sternly at the paper in his hands, 'that we are going to do everything we can to bring the perpetrators of this horrible crime to justice.'

'Thank you, David,' the major general answered. 'I know you'll do everything in your power.'

Littleton pushed his old friend's words away quickly as they brought back that nasty feeling of guilt that had been haunting him.

'The Ministry of Defence and the Foreign Office picked a wonderful pathologist. She has been very professional and extremely efficient.'

Littleton hated the words that came from his mouth as he couldn't stand the sight of Dr Laos.

'There's a lot of technical mumbo-jumbo in this document, which I won't bore you with,' he continued, thinking how best to avoid the cocaine issue, or at least how to contain the impact he knew it would have. 'Andrew was attacked and fatally wounded on his way back to the base in the early hours of Saturday morning. He had been out on a Friday night — as all of our young lads do when they have the time — you know, enjoying himself.'

The major general interrupted Littleton's rhetoric. 'Did Dr Laos say how and why Andrew was killed?'

Damn the blasted old fool, Littleton thought. *How he was killed? That I can answer. Why? That's a question I'd rather not. But no time like the present, I guess.*

The air vice-marshal poised himself and decided to give the information.

'Andrew appears to have been attacked by a blunt instrument that the pathologist says was the primary cause of death. He was also asphyxiated by his attacker by way of strangulation.'

Mrs Morrison started to cry. He ignored her, preferring to get this over and done with.

'There is something else you should know.' He looked at the Morrisons briefly and returned his glance to the autopsy report. 'The pathologist found a small packet of cocaine in Andrew's stomach during her autopsy.' He didn't pause to give the major general or his wife the chance to object. He saw their faces turn ashen.

'As for how it got there, that's anyone's guess, I'm sorry to say. However, I can assure you again that we are not going to let this case rest. Our Inspector Haws of the military police who heads up the criminal investigations department of this section of the Sovereign Base Areas is working very closely with the local police and Dr Laos to make some sense of Andrew's difficult death.'

'Cocaine?' spluttered the old major general. 'But why?'

The old fool hasn't heard a word I said, Littleton thought.

'Graham, I will get you the answers you need. But right now I think what's important is for you to take Andrew back home. Take some time for this tragedy to sink in and I am sure by then we will have apprehended the evil bastards that did this.'

'Of course,' the old man replied sullenly. He reached out his hand to shake that of the air vice-marshal. Littleton reciprocated, his hand shaky and sweaty. Major General Morrison didn't notice. Littleton then ushered the couple out of his office, again offering all the assurances he could think of in order to get the grieving parents out of his way.

He moved back to his desk just as his fax machine started coming to life. He watched as it slowly spilled a single sheet of A4 paper onto his desk. He lifted it up. It was from London. *It's the damn budgetary approval Dr Laos and Inspector Haws insisted on for drug screening. How dare he threaten me with a military court?* The air vice-marshal recalled the inspector's ultimatum from the previous day. He gathered his belongings, the fax from London and the coffee that sat still warm on his desk and headed out of his office. He quickly called into his secretary's office to hand her the fax so that Dr Laos and Inspector Haws could start their drug-screening schedule. His secretary sat motionless in her desk chair and looked as if she had seen a ghost.

'What's wrong with you this morning?' asked Littleton, unsympathetically.

'There's been another death,' she said, her eyes meeting his and hoping for some leadership and support.

Littleton almost dropped his coffee. 'What? When?' he asked, spluttering his words almost incoherently.

'One of the officer cadets. Suicide. A cleaner found him hanging in his wardrobe this morning.

'Where?' growled the air vice-marshal.

'In block B6 of the Officer Cadets' Barrack. Inspector Haws and Dr Laos are on their way there already.'

'Why the hell wasn't I told first?'

'You were . . . busy. With the parents of Lieutenant Morrison. I was about to call you,' she pleaded.

'Never mind that. I've got to get over there.'

He turned his back and started to walk out. She called after him. 'Sir, there's something else.'

What the hell's going on here? Littleton asked himself, fearing that his past and the secrets therein were getting closer to biting him in the arse.

'One of the other officer cadets is missing.'

Wednesday 22 August, 8:20 a.m.
Officer Cadets' Barrack; Block B6
Episkopi Garrison
Western Sovereign Base Area
Cyprus

Dr Laos had been awoken with the news of the death of Officer Cadet Phil Wakely by Inspector Chris Haws banging on her bedroom door. It had been the first decent sleep that Karen had had since she had arrived on the island. She knew instinctively that there had been another death; she could tell by the inspector's impassioned facial expression when she had opened the door to him. She quickly got dressed and by 7.50 a.m. had arrived with the inspector at the crime scene.

Junior officers from his team had been instructed not to move the victim's body until Dr Laos arrived. They had therefore simply secured the crime scene in anticipation of her arrival. *Second day on the job and it feels like it's becoming a full-time occupation already,* Karen had thought.

Upon their arrival, Inspector Haws had instructed his officers to leave the room and ensure that other soldiers were not given access to the building. A small group had started forming outside and was growing larger by the minute. Alone in the room, Karen turned to speak to Inspector Haws.

'Inspector, this is not the way I was planning to start my morning. There is something seriously amiss on this base and the sooner we get a handle on it the better.'

He thought she sounded angry. He moved aside to let her examine the body of Phil Wakely and just as he did so Air Vice-Marshal Littleton came trotting into the room, his face again red and sweaty. He opened his mouth to speak but Inspector Haws indicated to him to remain silent. He pointed to Dr Laos as she swung open the wardrobe door. She placed a pair of surgical gloves on her hands and reached inside the wardrobe. She pulled out a Dictaphone from her pocket and hit record.

'The victim's body is suspended from an anchor point by a ligature, which, on first impression, appears to be a tie. The position of the victim's neck suggests that he died by suspension hanging, also known as partial suspension.'

Karen moved her hands to where the ligature point formed into a lock at the victim's airway.

'The ligature is one that is commonly seen in cases of suicide by suspension hanging. The tie appears to have been tied into a noose, which in turn has been adjusted into an effective slip-knot, which would have been easily tightened upon the victim suspending himself. The position of the victim's body suggests that he died in three stages; compression of the carotid artery, followed by compression of the jugular vein and finally the airway. Time of death will be determined during autopsy. Additional blood work and further pathological analysis will be conducted. The current time is now 8.30 a.m.'

She turned her Dictaphone off and stood up to talk to Inspector Haws. Air Vice-Marshal Littleton looked anxious, so she nodded good morning to him and spoke to the two of them.

'Inspector, please have your officers remove the body and take it to the mortuary. I will need to run some further tests.'

Littleton stepped forward. 'My secretary told me that another of the officer cadets is missing. What is his name?'

Inspector Haws replied. 'This room was shared by Officer Cadets Phil Wakely, our latest victim, and Danny Mills. It is Mr Mills that appears to be missing. I have asked my officers to start a search of the bases area. We will also check CCTV footage from all entry and exit points.'

'Do you suspect foul play?' asked Littleton.

Dr Laos intervened. 'Mr Littleton. We have a case of what appears to be suicide. There is always a certain amount of what you may call 'foul play' in any suicide. However, if you are asking whether it is possible that Mr Wakely has been murdered, I would have to say at this point that I do not believe so. This looks like a classic case of suicide. You have to understand the psychology behind suicide. It is twofold. It can either be impulsive or planned. I would need to access Mr Wakely's medical file to ascertain whether there were any known risk factors that may have led to him killing himself. It is important also to keep in mind that suicide doesn't strictly refer to the process of killing oneself when taken alone. It is usually the final step in a long set of circumstances that leads the perpetrator to complete the suicide process.'

'That's very insightful, Dr Laos,' answered Air Vice-Marshal Littleton, acerbically. 'However, it makes no sense to me whatsoever as to why a young soldier would take his own life.'

'Don't be so sure of yourself, Mr Littleton,' replied Karen, riling the field officer more than she had previously. 'These are young cadets far away from their homes and families. None of us know the reasons why people ultimately finalize the process of completing suicide. Don't forget, the death of Andrew Morrison has caused a great deal of shock here on the base and there are a lot of unanswered questions, on the minds of many people. Add to that the murder last year of John Riley and the apparent drug problem, and I am sure that there are many on this base who wish they were as far away as possible.'

The air vice-marshal looked livid. 'I don't need you telling me what's going on in my own jurisdiction, thank you very much.'

Karen was unaffected by his words. 'You may not think so, Mr Littleton but your superiors at the Ministry of Defence obviously disagree with the way you have managed the situation here.'

She knew that she was treading on thin ice but didn't care any more. She felt sick of Littleton's patronizing and unprofessional method of working. Littleton turned and headed out of the room, his face now glowing with rage. As he left he shouted behind him, 'And for the record, Dr Laos, your funding has been approved — I suggest you start your drug-screening agenda.'

Karen called after him, 'Well noted, Mr Littleton. It is already in my diary for today.'

Dr Rebekah Terrobias had been circling around the room waiting for her chance to enter. As Littleton disappeared from view, she walked through the door with three of Inspector Haw's young officers.

She nodded at Dr Laos and Inspector Haws.

'We are here to remove the body of Mr Wakely.'

'Thank you, Rebekah,' Karen replied. 'Please have the body ready in the mortuary. I will be there shortly.'

She turned back to Inspector Haws.

'Let's take a walk, Inspector.'

He nodded and followed her out of the room. They walked down the stairs and exited the building. When they were clear of any eavesdroppers, he addressed Dr Laos.

'You certainly say what's on your mind, Dr Laos. I don't think I've ever seen the air vice-marshal so incensed by anybody before.'

'In that case,' said Karen, as they started walking to the mortuary, 'I will take that as a compliment. I am purposefully annoying him, Inspector. I don't trust that man for a minute and I don't know why but I think he is involved in all of this somehow.'

'That's a hell of a thing to say, Dr Laos. You do know that?'

'Of course I do, Inspector. I don't know how that man is involved but every instinct I have tells me he is. I'm purposefully annoying him in the hope that he will break and let something slip.'

'Even if you're right, he's cleverer than that,' said the inspector.

'We'll see, Inspector,' Karen replied. 'Now, as I was saying before I was so rudely interrupted by Mr Littleton, there are a number of factors you need to know about why people kill themselves. I'm only telling you this because I believe that the information will help with your investigations. The completion of suicide requires both a desire for death and a capability for lethal self-harm. We need to consider why Mr Wakely had such a desire. In many cases, the desire comes about when the suicidal individual has the perception that he or she is a great burden to family and friends or others and is usually accompanied by a low sense of belonging. Such feelings may not be valid but the individual strongly believes them to be so. These conditions can occur when someone experiences extreme hopelessness and helplessness and comes to feel that nothing or no one can help them. We are usually protected against suicide by our innate, instinctual desire for self-survival. Hopelessness and helplessness enable the suicidal individual to overcome these inhibitions against self-harm and suicide.'

Inspector Haws thought about what Dr Laos had told him. 'So, you are suggesting that we need to look for something, perhaps an event or situation, that led Mr Wakely into such a state?'

'Indeed, I am, Inspector. I would predict that something of a traumatic nature happened to the young man. We need to find out what that event was. We also need to find

189

the whereabouts of his missing friend and companion, young Mr Danny Mills. If Mr Mills found Phil Wakely hanging, he will no doubt be experiencing a range of difficult emotions. He will be what we call a 'suicide griever'; suicide is a sudden, traumatic and often violent end to one's life. It is also still highly stigmatized. We must therefore tread very carefully. Mr Mills will no doubt be experiencing guilt and be carrying round a great deal of anger, towards not only himself but Mr Wakely and possibly others. At this stage we can only assume that Mr Mills found Phil Wakely's body. Until you have the results from CCTV and the local area searches, we are working on the hypothesis that Danny Mills fled after finding Phil Wakely's body.'

Inspector Haws stopped walking and turned to Karen. 'Dr Laos, given what you have said, I think that my time will be better spent involved in the search for Danny Mills. How about we meet up again at midday? That will give you the time you need to conduct a formal autopsy on Mr Wakely. It will also allow me to track CCTV footage and hopefully find Mr Mills sooner, rather than later. I'm also going to arrange for the sniffer dogs to come onto the base; not only for helping in finding Danny Mills but also to find any sources of illicit drugs.'

'That sounds like a good idea, Inspector, but will the air vice-marshal agree to you bringing sniffer dogs onto the base?'

'If he doesn't, I will simply borrow your technique,' joked Inspector Haws, adding, 'or, of course, I'll simply threaten him with the military court again. It worked last time.'

Karen laughed. 'In that case, I will see you at midday. Good luck.'

15

Officer Cadet Danny Mills had moved quickly during the previous afternoon, having evaded detection in leaving Episkopi Garrison. He had stuck to back roads and whenever he had seen signs of a vehicle had hidden himself in bushes. He knew that he was in great danger, not only if he were caught and found by the cops but also from those he most feared. Sergii Filatov had already threatened his life once. He didn't want to be the third dead body related to whatever the hell was going on in under a week. First his mate Andrew Morrison had been murdered; yesterday his close friend Phil had topped himself. He was still reeling in shock about finding his dead friend. He also knew that there were other, more subtle dangers in his midst.

In the eighteen hours that he had been wandering around the fields and beaches

192

adjacent to Episkopi Garrison, Danny Mills had seen several large native black snakes. He had been told to simply stay put if he ever came face-to-face with a snake. He had also been told that the black snake, although not lethal, had a nasty habit of chasing people when scared, and whipping them with its tail, which those who had suffered the fate had described as being akin to a lashing with a razor blade. The far more dangerous snake that Danny knew lurked in the area was the fearsome Cypriot blunt-nosed viper, which had caused the death of several people over the past decade. He had been grateful when the sun had finally set the night before and darkness had fallen across the island. He knew that snakes were reptiles and therefore only likely to be laying directly on main paths and roads when the sun was high in the sky. Although snakes were active hunters by night in the summer months, lying in wait for passing rodents and cockroaches, Danny hadn't needed the shelter of the bushes for cover as the dark sky had provided more than enough camouflage. He reasoned that he would be safe out of the way of any predatory snakes as long as he stuck to the main roads. During the night he had managed to cross a large distance and had stopped in the village of Kolossi at 9 p.m. the previous night.

He had felt grateful when the sun had finally set as his shoulders were red and sore from the early-evening sun. He remembered that aloe vera, which grew wild and in ample supply on the island, had been reputed to be among the best remedies for sunburn. With this in mind, he had broken a small piece of the plant and squeezed the pulp inside into the palm of his hands. He had rubbed it on his shoulders and felt the relief almost immediately.

Kolossi was a small village populated pre-dominantly by the local population. Danny had felt tired and decided to find somewhere to rest. He had come upon the village church, which was unlocked and deserted. Inside he found a natural spring, under which a sign said in English and Greek that the water was safe to drink. He had been extremely thirsty and had drunk from the spring for ten min-utes straight. Danny then found a long wooden congregational bench and lay down. The church was far cooler than his room at the base had ever been. He started to fall asleep and had no clue as to where he would head thereafter.

★   ★   ★

The Cyprus Joint Police Unit, headed up by Inspector Andreou, had contributed to the search for Officer Cadet Danny Mills at the request of Inspector Chris Haws. Haws and his team had taken the front over a standard grid search pattern, leading out in all directions from the exits of Episkopi Garrison, and backing up on itself, ensuring that all known coded areas that fell under the map they had plotted out would be sufficiently covered. The advantage of the grid search meant that it was especially effective for searching large areas. Chris Haws had spent an hour and a half supervising the search but had so far failed to find any tangible leads that would bring them any closer to locating Officer Cadet Mills. He therefore returned to Episkopi Garrison and started the process of questioning gatemen and checking CCTV footage that had been shot at the entrances and exits over the last twenty-four hours.

Inspector Andreou had supervised his own team of local police, whom he had instructed to comb surrounding villages and question local residents by knocking on doors and presenting a photograph of Danny Mills that had been provided by the base's personnel files. He had of course a level of his own self-interest in finding Danny Mills; he suspected that his disappearance and Phil Wakely's death might be related. If Phil

Wakely's death was in turn related to the death of Andrew Morrison, he would find himself one step closer to forming the link he needed with Charlie Charalambos and possibly Sergii Filatov.

Andreou had completed his own search of two villages before he had arrived in Kolossi. He knew that if Officer Cadet Mills had travelled by foot, as the police suspected, he would have been able by now to have covered a lot of ground. The search wasn't being made any easier by not knowing at what time Mills had left the base. If Dr Laos were able to quickly determine a time of death, their chances of locating the young soldier would be helped by the fact that they assumed Danny Mills had fled after discovering his friend's body. After knocking on countless doors in the village, each drawing a blank, Andreou began to have some worrying thoughts. *What if someone's got to him? If Filatov or Charalambos are involved, the kid could be dead by now. Sure, I've got a trace going on Charalambos, but Filatov is as slippery and elusive as always.*

His mobile phone buzzed in his trouser pocket. He saw that Inspector Haws was calling him.

'Where are you, Dimitris?' asked Haws.

'I'm in Kolossi. I don't see that Danny

Mills could have got much further than here, if he travelled by foot. Have you had any leads your end?' He waited for the inspector to reply.

'Well, I haven't heard anything from Dr Laos yet, but I've been checking the CCTV. It looks as if young Danny left the base at 4.25 p.m. yesterday afternoon. I'm at the civilian entrance. The gatemen on duty yesterday afternoon didn't see him go. I only spotted him on the film when I played it back for the third time. He sneaked up behind a row of eucalyptus trees and ran across the road. That means he's been travelling on foot for about eighteen hours, give or take time for resting up. The image we managed to pull up is pretty grainy but it looks like he's dressed in just a T-shirt, shorts and wearing flip-flops. He would be hard pressed to get anywhere fast. I think you're about right in targeting Kolossi. Keep checking and let me know. As soon as I hear from Dr Laos, I'll give you a call.'

'Understood,' said Andreou. 'Are we still on for midday?'

'We are,' replied Haws. 'Instruct your officers to meet at Gatehouse number one on the base. I will give them further directions at that time.'

★   ★   ★

Despite having woken up several times during the night, Danny Mills had slept better than he thought that he would. Each time he had woken up, he had returned to the natural water spring and drunk several more mouthfuls of water. He hadn't needed the toilet and realized just how dehydrated he had been by the trip he had made the previous night. The sound of the church bells ringing out loudly across the village had frightened him in the early hours. He thought he was about to be found by a bell-ringer or the priest but had soon realized that the bells were working automatically on a timer: there was no one physically ringing them. He had looked several times for an opportunity to leave the church, but each time he had tried to he had been prevented, as the street outside always seemed to be full. Between 6 a.m. and 8.30 a.m., the road had been full of commuting traffic.

Danny tried to remember where Kolossi was located. He recalled that the village fell between the main highway and the one and only road that led down from villages higher up in the mountains. That put him slap-bang in the middle of commuter traffic, heading north to south from villages at high altitude, such as Agios Ambrosios down to Limassol to the east or Paphos to the west. It also put the village at the centre of outlying village commuters travelling along the main A1 highway to either Limassol or Paphos. When the traffic had died down, Danny had looked out of one of the windows and seen a street market coming to life.

He thought it might be his best chance to move unnoticed through the crowds, but as he had stepped out onto the street, he quickly did a U-turn and went back inside. A Cyprus Joint Police Unit patrol car had slowly been making its way along the street. He watched from inside as Inspector Andreou made his way from door to door.

Wednesday 22 August, 11.25 a.m.
S.B.A Medical Facility — Clinical Labora-
*   tory*
Episkopi Garrison
Western Sovereign Base Area
Cyprus

'Do you ever get used to this, Dr Laos?' asked Rebekah Terrobias as Karen was sitting at a small desk typing her latest autopsy findings on her laptop.

'Get used to what, Rebekah?' she answered.

Rebekah lifted her left hand and pointed to the lifeless body of Officer Cadet Phil Wakely.

Karen stopped typing.

'I wouldn't say that it's something I ever take for granted, if that's what you mean. I try not to ever forget the names of the people that I have performed an autopsy on; that is, where their names are available, of course. But, yes, it is inevitable that I have developed a clinical relationship with the individuals, even though they are dead. If I think too much about the job I do, I guess I wouldn't be very good at it. I simply do it. You have to remember, Rebekah, especially in cases like murder or suicide, that your job as the pathologist is to write the final chapter of the book of the individual's life that you're examining.'

Dr Terrobias looked thoughtful. 'That's a nice analogy, Dr Laos. What do you say in that final chapter?'

Karen stood up from behind the desk she had been sitting at.

'I report my findings. I hope that the conclusion I give will bring some peace and closure to those that the deceased has left behind. It isn't always the case. There have been times in my career when I have struggled to make sense of that final chapter in a person's life.'

She walked over to where Phil Wakely lay on the pedestal-style autopsy table.

'Mr Wakely, for example: how do we conclude the last chapter of his life? What is it that made him end his life so violently and so suddenly? If the deceased could speak, what would he tell us about why he did what he did?' She looked at Rebekah. 'Don't worry. I'm not expecting actual answers to those metaphysical questions, Dr Terrobias. I'm simply trying to answer your initial question. We want to be able to give the family of this young man something that they will be able to understand. They may not be able to make much sense of his actions immediately, but with time we hope they can. Take Mr Morrison, for example. The autopsy was completed; by all accounts it seems pretty grim. He was taking drugs, smuggling them into the base and ultimately paid the greatest price: he was killed. Where do you think his family will find peace and answers in that?'

'I think they will only find peace if we can bring their son's killer to justice.'

'Exactly,' replied Dr Laos. 'Now, what do you say you help me write the final chapter of Phil Wakely's life?'

'How can I do that?' asked Dr Terrobias. 'You've completed your autopsy already.'

'True. But it sometimes helps if a colleague reads back to me what I have written. Would you mind doing that?'

Karen knew that in reading the findings out loud, her young colleague would better understand the point that she was trying to make. Rebekah Terrobias walked around to where Karen's laptop sat and started reading.

'I, the undersigned medical officer and Consultant Forensic Pathologist, Dr Karen Laos, hereby find that Officer Cadet Philip Wakely died as a result of self-inflicted partial-suspension hanging. The victim, aged twenty-one years at the time of death, was found on the morning of Wednesday 22 August by a domestic member of staff based at Episkopi Garrison. The victim's body was not, to the best of my professional determination or knowledge, interfered with after the time of his death. Initial post-mortem examination would suggest that the victim died at approximately 1 p.m. on Tuesday 21 August. This is consistent with the stage of rigor mortis that the victim's body had reached by the time he was discovered. It must be noted that rigor mortis in this case is not an exact science or predictor of the time of death due to the high environmental temperatures and humidity in the room in which the victim was found. Such conditions have been found to affect the stages of rigor mortis.

'I, Dr Karen Laos, attended the scene of

death along with Inspector Chris Haws, immediately upon hearing of the incident. I arrived at 8.20 a.m. and recorded preliminary details gleaned from external examination. These details were recorded verbally and will be included at the end of this report. My findings during the autopsy include the fact that the victim fashioned a tie into an improvised noose and finalized the act of suicide by partially suspending himself from a ligature point inside a bedroom wardrobe. The effects of partial suspension are three-fold; the victim would have entered a state of semi-consciousness upon the commencement of the compression of his carotid arteries. Internal examination confirms the same.

'The victim's jugular veins and airway are also in a state consistent with the effects of death by partial suspension. The victim's body weight suggests that about 5kg of pressure was required to compress the carotid artery; 2kg for the jugular veins; and at least 15kg for the airway to be compressed. This is consistent with the position in which the victim's body was found. Internal examination of the remainder of the victim's body is not, in a case of death via this method, either required or desirable.'

'Very enlightening,' said Dr Terrobias after she had read Dr Laos' report.

'It is indeed, Rebekah, especially if you scroll down to the next page. I have entered there some blood-work results as well as a sample of the victim's urine, which I extracted during examination.'

Rebekah Terrobias did as suggested. 'Oh, God,' she exclaimed. 'I didn't think about that.'

'Please, read it aloud,' continued Karen.

' 'Blood-work pathology indicates that the victim had ingested, either willingly or unwillingly, high levels of cocaine prior to his death. Cocaine is extensively metabolized, primarily in the liver, with only about 1 per cent excreted unchanged in the urine. The metabolism is dominated by hydrolytic ester cleavage, so the eliminated metabolites consist mostly of benzoylmethylecgonine, the major metabolite, and in lesser amounts ecgonine methyl ester and ecgonine.

' 'Depending on liver and kidney function, cocaine metabolites are detectable in urine, as is the case in the current investigation. Benzoylmethylecgonine can be detected in urine within four hours after cocaine intake and remains detectable in concentrations greater than 150ng/ml typically for up to eight days after cocaine is used. A sample of the victim's hair also confirms that he had used the drug. A best clinical deduction would put such use at within the window of twelve hours prior to death.

''Preliminary conclusive comments must state that I have examined the victim's medical records available on his military personnel files. There is no mention of, or history indicated of, previous substance abuse. At this stage, I must conclude that the trend towards the cocaine misuse currently affecting Episkopi Garrison is correlated, that is to say that the deaths of both Lieutenant Andrew Morrison and Officer Cadet Phil Wakely are related insofar as their deaths occurred within seventy-two hours of one another and that both victims have tested positive for cocaine. They differ in that Lieutenant Andrew Morrison died as a result of murder, and Mr Wakely died as a result of suicide.

''Given the fact that Mr Wakely's medical files show no history of a predisposition to mental illness or any other major factor that can be related to suicide or drug use, I would surmise that he had an extreme, although rare, psychological reaction to the use of cocaine, which placed him in a vulnerable state of mind prior to his taking his own life. It will be for ongoing police investigations to determine the nature of the circumstances in which the victim found himself taking cocaine. It must also be noted on record that it is the opinion of the reporting medical officer that the victim was exposed to a traumatic experience in the hours prior to his death. Such an experience, when amplified physically and mentally by the psychoactive effects of cocaine, could have resulted in the victim's decision to end his life.''

'So,' said Dr Laos. 'The importance of our being able to write that final chapter of the victim's life is evident. What's important now is to close any gaps of circumspection that may be in that report.' She pointed to the laptop. 'We can start on that by getting these results to Inspector Haws as soon as possible. The sooner we find Mr Wakely's missing friend, Danny Mills, the sooner we can hopefully put a satisfactory end to this case.'

She reached for her mobile phone and called Chris Haws. Rebekah Terrobias was lost in thought, and quite awestruck by both Karen's objectivity and the personal touches that she had added to the autopsy report. She hadn't seen that previously in a consultant's work. She overheard Dr Laos on the phone confirming the time of death, the cause of death and of course the fact that cocaine had played a role.

Just before Dr Laos ended the call, Rebekah also heard her say that she would fax a copy of the report to the inspector's office, that of Inspector Andreou and, more out of politeness and duty than respect, to the air vice-marshal's secretary. She also confirmed that she would meet the inspector at 1 p.m. in the canteen.

16

Wednesday 22 August, 12 p.m.
Military Entrance Gatehouse No. 1
Episkopi Garrison
Western Sovereign Base Area
Cyprus

A large congregation of both military police and officers from the Cyprus Joint Police Unit were gathering at the main entrance of Episkopi Garrison. Their vehicles had backed up along the entrance road as each police officer awaited instructions and clearance at the gatehouse. In total, thirty officers from across the island's ninety-six square miles of British Sovereign Base Area had assembled and were waiting for further directions from Inspector Chris Haws, who was overseeing the operation. He had acted as soon as the funding approval for the commencement of drug screenings had come through.

Inspector Andreou had released a further fifteen of his own officers for the day. He had also provided a total of five sniffer dogs from his unit; three Labradors and two German shepherds. Each dog stood eagerly with its own trainer. They had been uniquely trained to detect substances such as explosives, illegal drugs and human blood. Several officers from the base's own Military Police Division had also been asked to arrive for duty today with their own dogs. These were dogs that had formed strong attachments to their handlers and had undergone specialized training from the time they were puppies. In both the military and police units, they were considered 'part of the family' and a single loss of any detection dog whilst in action was traditionally mourned in the same way that that of a fallen human comrade would be.

Each of the forty-five police and military police officers was equipped with standard issue double-action, semi-automatic Smith & Wesson pistols. Whilst it was normal practice for all police in Cyprus to carry firearms, the British military police were distinguished from their colleagues in police forces on non-military duty that did not carry firearms. The Smith & Wesson model that all the officers carried today had been introduced in 2005. It weighed 700 grams and had a magazine capacity of 9mm and 15 rounds. It had been constructed from a high-strength polymer frame and a stainless-steel barrel and side; it made for an impressive sight. It was also highly functional, with a neat sear release lever that could be easily released without the striker having to pull the trigger. Both front and rear sights were dovetailed to the side and could therefore be readily adjusted and replaced by the optional tritium night-sights.

Inspector Haws watched from the inside of the gatehouse as he finalized plans for the day with his colleagues. Air Vice-Marshal Littleton had buzzed around nervously for the past twenty minutes interfering with Inspector Haws' plans for the manner in which the day would pan out.

'What's that?' he had asked, looking over the inspector's shoulder.

'That's my planning, sir, for the teams that I am drawing up.'

'Is that really necessary?' pressed the air vice-marshal.

'Yes, sir, it is. I need to allocate the resources we have in the best possible manner. I'm working alone until Inspector Andreou gets back from his search for the missing officer cadet. I also need Dr Laos, Dr Terrobias and some of the nurses to oversee the drug-screening process.'

Littleton chose to ignore the last part of the inspector's words. He leaned in close to Inspector Haws.

'How is Andreou getting on with finding young Danny Mills?'

His voice was nervy but Inspector Haws was too preoccupied to pick up on it. He naively assumed that the air vice-marshal was trying to show some genuine concern.

'No reported sign of him yet, sir.'

'Well, let's hope all's well that ends well, yes?'

The air vice-marshal tapped Chris Haws on the shoulder, adding, 'Keep me updated, will you, as soon as there is any development on the search efforts?'

Haws shot a look at the air vice-marshal. 'I always do, sir.'

'Yes, quite right, Inspector, but just make sure that you do this time. I need to speak to the young officer cadet as soon as he is located, given what Dr Laos found.'

He was referring of course to the positive identification of cocaine in Phil Wakely's autopsy. Before Inspector Haws had the chance to respond, the air vice-marshal walked out and headed back to his office.

Wednesday 22 August, 12.20 p.m.
Kolossi Village
Western Sovereign Base Area
Cyprus

Although he usually stood out like a gaping hole on the landscape, today Little Sam had been told by his boss Sergii to 'blend in'. He had done his best by dressing as a tourist. His large frame had been squeezed into a tight pair of knee-length red shorts, brown sandals for his feet, white socks to his knees and his considerable gut, less easy to disguise, pulled into a blue T-shirt. Sergii had laughed at him as he had left in the morning.

'Be careful, Little Sam 'cos some old Cypriot broad might take a shining to you!' he had boomed. He had soon after dropped his jovial tone. 'I need you to blend in like a tourist; be the fat Russian you are.'

Stanislav Young, a male of twenty-four years old, had been planted at the British Bases by Sergii Filatov and Charlie Charalambos. Sergii had sourced and provided Stanislav, who was of Russian and British descent, and Charlie had managed, with his manipulation of Air Vice-Marshal David Littleton, to get him a civilian position on the base. He had proven himself very useful ever since Sergii and Charlie had gone into business together. He kept a relatively low profile as a gateman at the civilian entrance, working the late-night and early-morning shift pattern in rotation.

He was pleased with his job; a double salary by way of his work on the side for Sergii and Charlie. The more information he provided them with, the higher the interest they paid him on his basic wage; the wage he took from his employment as a gateman was minimal. He had called Sergii late Tuesday night after he had taken over his watch on the night shift to say that he had successfully managed to get the two young officer cadets back into the base that morning, following their little adventure into Limassol's Colours Nightclub. Sergii had been pleased with Stanislav's work, but had warned him to keep a close eye on the two young soldiers.

Sergii's satisfaction with Stanislav's work had soon turned to anger and abuse. It had been shortly before 8 a.m. on Wednesday morning that Stanislav had heard that Danny Mills had gone missing. Stanislav panicked, fearing that he would be punished by Sergii and Charlie when he told them what had happened.

'What the fuck do I pay you for?' Sergii had shouted down the phone at him, switching between Russian and English in his rage. 'Are you trying to make me look stupid? I swear I'll be coming for you if you don't sort this mess out.'

Stanislav didn't know what to do and had apologized to his boss, of whom he was petrified. Sergii had told him to keep his ears to the ground and stay awake and to let him know what the British were going to do to locate the missing soldier. At the end of a long night, Stanislav had really wanted to get some sleep. But he also knew the consequences of not obeying his paymaster. He had slyly listened in on the developments of the morning; he had watched closely as Dr Karen Laos and Inspector Chris Haws had attended block B6 of the Officer Cadets' Barracks. He had heard them talking about their plans for the day and he had overheard sketchy details about the search that would be launched for Danny Mills.

He had relayed all of this information back to Sergii Filatov. Sergii didn't want to leave a 24-year-old in charge of this mess and had decided to send Little Sam to the area. Little Sam had quickly picked up on the scent of the cops looking for Danny Mills. He knew Inspector Andreou, having had several encounters with him over the years.

As soon as he had spotted Andreou busily moving through the market stalls and knocking on the neighbourhood doors, he had donned a large cap and shades and started to follow him at a distance of twenty metres, stopping and blending in at the market stalls each time he thought he might be getting too close. He watched as Inspector Andreou paused outside a kiosk. He went in briefly and came out with a refrigerated cold coffee. An old village church faced directly opposite where the inspector now stood, drinking from his tinned milk coffee.

Andreou stopped an elderly local man who was busy buying vegetables from a market seller. Little Sam was too far away to hear what he asked the old man but thought it might be something to do with the church as he saw the old man look at his watch and point in the direction of the church building. He then saw Andreou cross the road. Little Sam moved in closer at the same time as a large eighteen-wheeler truck carrying livestock from the mountains entered the street. People moved across the road to make way for the truck and in the unexpected crowd Little Sam temporarily lost sight of Andreou. He pushed his way forwards, trying to better see where the inspector had gone. The driver of the truck moved his vehicle slowly down the street, the brakes loud and noisy. The sound was not too dissimilar to that of a mushy, grinding noise.

Andreou looked at the door of the church. It seemed to be closed but he knew it wouldn't be locked. He pushed at the door until it opened, and stepped inside. He closed the door behind him. The large truck outside continued, its brakes dragging and scraping as it moved and stopped. The sound it made echoed along the length of the ancient street.

The church was dark and cooling. The inspector looked around.

'Danny,' he called. 'Are you in here?'

No answer.

'I'm Inspector Andreou, I'm here to help you.'

No answer.

Danny Mills sat still, crouched beneath an elevated and ornate pulpit. *Do I take my chances with this cop? Maybe it's best to wait till he's gone, but I can't stay here for ever.*

The truck outside continued crunching its way down the street. Little Sam was still trying to get a view of the church.

He hadn't seen where the inspector had gone and felt rattled that he might have lost him. A family of five crossed the street and stopped at the back end of the truck, waiting until it had moved out of their way. The parents clung tightly to their children, concerned by the noises that the vehicle was making. Little Sam started to cross the road, still looking for the inspector. He planned to go around the back of the church and see if there were any windows through which he could look. As he approached the centre of the road, a cyclist almost knocked him down. He instinctively turned to shout at the cyclist and as he did so, he heard the screeching of the truck's wheels coming from the opposite direction.

The noise was close and deafening. He twisted his body back to the direction the truck was coming from and felt a vertebra in his back click into a spasm. The pain was excruciating and immobilized him immediately.

He heard people shouting at him to move; he saw the driver of the vehicle waving frantically and heard the horn of the truck telling him to get the hell out of the road. He threw his hands in the air as the truck closed in on him. The last thing that Little Sam saw as he disappeared underneath the front of the truck was an assembly of gears and wheels. The sound of people screaming and shouting outside the church made Inspector Andreou turn back. He was about ready to exit the church when he heard the voice of a young man coming from the far end of the church.

'Inspector. Wait. I'm Danny Mills. I think I need to talk to you.'

Wednesday 22 August, 12.45 p.m.
Episkopi Garrison
Western Sovereign Base Area
Cyprus

Inspector Chris Haws had divided the officers in his charge into nine teams of five. He had purposefully mixed officers from his own

217

division of military police with those provided by the Cyprus Joint Police Unit. Of the fifteen officers that Inspector Andreou had provided, Chris Haws had decided to provide one to each of the nine teams. The remaining five officers were divided randomly among the nine teams. Each team had at least two sniffer dogs with them. Inspector Haws had explained to the officers as they stood waiting at the checkpoint entrance to Episkopi Garrison that their search would have three objectives.

'We will be working today as a united team. You have three objectives. The first is to find and locate illicit substances with the help of your working dogs. The second is to find clues that will assist us in our search for Officer Cadet Danny Mills. It is imperative that we find him both quickly and safely. Inspector Andreou is heading a smaller team searching for him on the perimeter of the bases area. I therefore want all officers working on the inside perimeter of the base. You will start here at Episkopi Garrison. When Episkopi has been searched, we will regroup and make plans for searching the remaining areas, if deemed necessary at that time. During the time in which you will be searching the base, I want all teams to remain in contact with one another at all times. Set your radios to the prefix of ZC4; I will hear all of your correspondence and will be monitoring everything that happens.'

The inspector studied the faces of the crowd that stood listening to him. He looked at each individually, quickly, and continued. 'Your third objective today is related to objective number one. All soldiers and military personnel have been instructed to gather at 3 p.m. at warehouse number five. You all know where that is. A team of nurses will be conducting urine test analyses of all military personnel. That includes those of you that are in the military police. The nurses will be overseen by Dr Rebekah Terrobias and Dr Karen Laos. They also have a full list of names of all military personnel currently serving at Episkopi Garrison. Our counterparts in the Eastern Sovereign Base Area will be conducting similar exercises over the next two days.

'If by 3 p.m. you find any soldiers not where they are allocated to be at warehouse number five, you are to instruct them to immediately make their way there without delay. All training exercises on the base have been halted until further notice. The base will also from this time forwards be closed to all incoming and outgoing military personnel. You have your orders. Let's get started.'

After the inspector had seen the officers into the garrison and all successfully pass security, he headed as planned to meet Dr Karen Laos. He was getting used to her company and appreciated being able to talk to her. He also admired her professionalism. As he approached the same staff canteen that he had previously sat in with Dr Laos, his mobile phone buzzed in his pocket. Inspector Andreou's voice was difficult to hear; there was a great deal of background noise.

'Chris,' he shouted. 'I've got good news. I'm with Danny Mills and we are coming back to the base.'

Inspector Haws felt relief pulsing through his body. 'That's great news, Dimitris. Well done. What's all that background noise?'

'That's the sound of another bit of good news. One of Sergii Filatov's boys was apparently tracking me. He's just been squashed to death in the middle of Kolossi village by an eighteen-wheeler truck.'

17

Air Vice-Marshal Littleton closed the curtains on all of his office windows and made sure that all doors leading in and out were locked. He called his secretary and told her that he didn't want to be disturbed for the next hour at least. David Littleton had plans and something urgent pressing on his guilty mind. He pulled a bunch of keys from out of his trouser pocket and located a small black key that he then proceeded to use to unlock the bottom drawer of his desk. He gave the drawer a tug. It had the habit of getting stuck after the old lock had been turned. It opened. Littleton reached inside and pulled out a grey padlocked box. He then located a further, smaller key and opened the padlock.

He lifted the box onto his desk and manoeuvered it open. Inside he found a small nylon bag and some sheets of paper. He held the paper in his hands and studied the black type font that detailed his offshore bank account in Beirut. He had requested to only receive bank statements every six months. The paper he now looked at represented far more than money, although the air vice-marshal didn't appreciate that fact. The interest on the money that the mob had paid to him over the years had accumulated into a tidy sum. *Illegal but tidy.* Littleton smiled as he thought about how clever he had been. Those bloody gangsters thought they had pulled one over on him. He liked the fact that they didn't know he had been taking an extra share of money from the gullible soldiers themselves and piping that through to his Beirut account.

It was only fair after all. He had allowed the mafia to use his base and his command for their nefarious dealings. Why shouldn't he make some extra bonus on top of that which they already paid him?

Littleton hadn't, however, on this occasion, only opened the box to study his wealth, although it did help with the plans that he had for his future. He had more urgent concerns today given the recent events that had taken place on his base. He had tried his best to distance himself from the investigations that Dr Laos and Inspector Haws were conducting right under his nose. He strongly disapproved of what they were doing as he feared that their investigations would lead back to his own role in everything that had been happening. As a seasoned soldier, he knew that he would be best placed to simply comply with the orders that had arrived over the past few days from his superiors in London. The arrival of a forensic pathologist was already bad enough for the air vice-marshal, especially one so damn opinionated as Dr Karen Laos. He had asked for a military pathologist when the MOD and Foreign Office had informed him of their plans. They had ignored his request.

At least he would have been able to maintain some control over a military doctor. He reasoned therefore that in order to divert attention away from his own command, he would stay as much as he could in the background. He had hidden his anger at the arrival of sniffer dogs and the involvement that Haws had invited of the Cyprus Joint Police Unit onto the base. He knew that it would be only a matter of time before the sniffer dogs and their handlers came into his office and private quarters as they rooted into every corner of the base. Inspector Haws wasn't listening to the opinions of his commanding officer and kept spouting on and on about how his true accountability lay with the military court and not in the laws of Littleton's own office. Littleton quickly realized that he had to step up his own game and protect his hand and the hands of those that fed him so much cash.

He placed the paperwork back into the grey box and reached instead for something else that he had safely hidden inside. It was a far larger key than that he had used to open the grey box, neatly concealed within the lining of the nylon bag. He removed it from inside the bag and walked to the far wall of his office. He struggled for a moment to move a metallic filing shelf that covered a safety deposit box that he had installed into the wall of his office. With the metallic filing cupboard out of his way, he went back to his desk and picked up the grey box. He closed it and placed the padlock back where it belonged. He reached down to the safety deposit box and inserted the much larger key. He turned it in an anticlockwise position and waited.

A vacuum seal released and he turned the key one more rotation to enable the door to swing open. It did so slowly. Littleton thought that it would open more quickly but then, he had only opened it once previously to test that it worked. He moved to reach his hand inside and felt a thick plastic screen preventing him from gaining access. He was taken aback so much so that he didn't move for ten seconds. The shock of having been locked out of his own safety deposit box left him breathless and confused. He slowly regained his composure and bent down on his knees to study the plastic screen that had blocked his access.

What the hell? How did this happen?

His initial shock gave way to anger as he realized that his office and personal space had been tampered with. He examined the plastic and realized that it was constructed of a tough piece of Perspex that had been intricately drilled into the interior of the safety deposit box.

He banged his fists against it in an effort to dislodge it. It was a useless and futile attempt as it had been so well inserted that it wasn't going anywhere. The reality of his situation dawned on Littleton as he realized that he had nowhere that he could hide the small grey padlocked box that had sat for so long in the bottom drawer of his desk. *You stupid fool. You had all these years to make sure it was concealed somewhere out of the way and you had to leave it until now?* He snapped himself out of self-blame. As he looked again at the thick layer of Perspex inserted into the interior of his own safety deposit box he saw for the first time something else. A note had been stuck on the inside of the thick sheet of Perspex.

'READ ME' it said in bold letters.

He moved his eyes over the piece of paper, following the instructions and invite that so boldly sat safely on the other side.

'Littleton; if you're reading this, your usefulness to us is over. We assume that you're panicking right about now. You should be! Look behind me; let's call it a present for the help you've provided over the years.'

The air vice-marshal looked behind where the note was stuck. He had to cup his hands to get a good view. He suddenly felt a cold, sickening chill move down his spine as he realized that behind the Perspex, safely out of his reach, lay two bags of neatly-wrapped cocaine.

Wednesday 22 August, 1 p.m.
Military Personnel Canteen No. 2
Episkopi Garrison
Western Sovereign Base Area
Cyprus

Dr Karen Laos and Inspector Chris Haws commandeered the same table they had sat at previously when they had met at the canteen. Karen hoped that their encounter this time would not be hampered by an interfering and aggressive Air Vice-Marshal Littleton. She had arrived at the same time as Chris Haws. The base was extremely busy and Karen had passed several groups of armed police, replete with sniffer dogs, on her way to the canteen. Despite the number of additional personnel walking around, there was an odd serenity on the base. Karen assumed that this was perhaps a result of nerves and of course the recent disturbing murder of Lieutenant Andrew Morrison and the suicide of Officer Cadet Phil Wakely.

'You're not drinking coffee, Dr Laos?' the inspector asked as he made himself comfortable in a chair.

'No, Inspector, I thought I'd have something more refreshing today.'

She indicated the orange juice that sat in front of her. The inspector leaned in close to Karen Laos and lowered his voice.

'Doctor, there is something I need to tell you,' he started.

Karen looked at him and moved in to meet his expression.

'Inspector Andreou has successfully located Danny Mills. He is on his way back to the base now. I just this minute called him and told him to wait outside the base until further instruction. He said he'd take Danny somewhere to get something to eat. I'm in somewhat of a difficult position. I should have informed Air Vice-Marshal Littleton as soon as Danny was found, but I didn't.'

'That could be problematic,' Karen agreed. 'But I think I know why you didn't tell the air vice-marshal.'

'Really?' asked Haws.

'You said it yourself, Inspector. You don't trust the man. You used to think that that feeling of distrust arose out of the air vice-marshal being somewhat quirky. But now you don't. Something has changed. Tell me what it is, Inspector Haws.'

'It's something you said. It stayed on my mind ever since. I can't stop thinking about it. I watched the way that you tackled Littleton about his attitude to implementing the drug screens and the way that he reacted to you. His whole reaction seemed disproportionate to what you were telling him. If it were simply a case of his disagreeing with you, he should have said so. But the way he acted came across as if you had personally offended him.'

Karen nodded. 'You're wondering whether your trust in the air vice-marshal has been wrongly placed. You also feel concerned that he may be involved somehow in everything that's been going on over recent days. That's the only logical reason you would refrain from informing your own commanding officer that Danny Mills had been found.'

Inspector Haws raised his eyebrows. 'You're good, Dr Laos. Very good. How do you suggest I proceed?'

'Well, what would be the normal procedure in cases such as this?' asked Karen.

'You mean, in cases where I have no trust in the integrity of my own commanding officer? I would need to have some evidence to back up my actions. All I have right now is a gut feeling that he is somehow involved. I'm afraid that a gut feeling isn't going to wash with the MOD.'

Karen thought about the situation the inspector was in before she replied. 'Well, you have one advantage.'

'What's that?' enquired the inspector.

'Time is on your side. Danny Mills is safe. He might know something that could help you. I'd suggest you play the fool for now. Don't tell the air vice-marshal that Danny Mills is safe. Wait until you've spoken to him. He might be willing to shed some light on what happened to Phil Wakely that made him take his life. Wait until the bigger picture has been formed; let the sniffer dogs and their handlers do their job. See what happens; then make your mind up. If the air vice-marshal is innocent in all of this, simply say that you were very busy with overseeing the operations here on the base and apologize for not informing him sooner.'

'You're very smart, Dr Laos. I think I will follow your advice. How about you? How are you holding up?'

Karen thought that his question was sweet, but unnecessary. 'I'm fine, Inspector. Thanks for asking. We both have busy days ahead of us. The autopsy on Phil Wakely didn't turn up anything that unexpected. I haven't been able to entirely conclude my autopsy report yet. There are certain areas that need filling in. For example, I know that he used cocaine in the hours leading up to his death. I also know that the cocaine he used is from the same source as was used by Andrew Morrison. What I don't know is from where he obtained the drug and indeed where he took it. I don't get the impression that it was used in the room where his body was found. I am hoping that Danny Mills can fill in those gaps.'

'I'll make sure you're involved in the meeting I have with Mr Mills,' the inspector assured Karen.

'I think it's best if when we see him, he doesn't feel that we are out to get him or to punish him. He's obviously going to be feeling frightened and scared enough already,' Karen said.

The inspector paused as he recalled that he had forgotten to let Dr Laos know something else. 'Oh, Inspector Andreou also told me that he thinks he was being followed by one of Sergii Filatov's boys. Not only did Andreou manage to find Danny Mills. He was also witness to a road traffic fatality. He identified the victim as one of Filatov's guys.'

'That answers another question,' replied Karen.

'What's that?' asked Inspector Haws.

'Inspector Andreou said that he wanted to know who the Russian was that Charlie Charalambos boasted about working with. You just told me that one of Filatov's boys had been following Andreou and came to a sudden and ferocious end. I'd say that's a pretty damning link between Filatov's involvement with the base and possibly the murder of Andrew Morrison and the suicide of Phil Wakely. Now, my question to you is, how do you plan to prove all of this?'

The inspector looked thoughtfully at Dr Laos. 'I have a few ideas. But they all depend on whether we can count on Danny Mills to help us out.'

Wednesday 22 August, 1.40 p.m.
Kolossi Village
Western Sovereign Base Area
Cyprus

Inspector Dimitris Andreou had been some-what torn in his duties when Danny Mills had unexpectedly stepped forward from the shadows of the cool church. The sound of Little Sam's obliteration under the wheels of the truck in the street outside had initially pulled him to get the hell out there and do what a cop was supposed to do: sort the mess out; radio other emergency services and generally try to bring the street back to its previously peaceful and mundane state. The sight of Danny Mills, however, had left the inspector fixed in one place.

'Danny,' he had said. 'I'm so pleased to see you alive and well.'

He didn't know the young soldier person-ally but certainly understood the importance of locating him. Danny, on the other hand, felt far more apprehensive about going off with the inspector. He knew that he would be safer than he was if he simply continued to run. He had realized after his night of relatively good sleep that he was faced with two options: the first was to return to the base and hand himself in. He didn't feel too comfortable with doing that, considering what he had heard from Sergii Filatov about the death of Andrew Morrison. He suspected that there was something far more sinister at play back at Episkopi Garrison.

The second option he had seen was to return to Limassol and track down Sergii Filatov again, hoping that he would provide him with some protection. Danny Mills had even thought that Sergii might be pleased that he had shown such trust in him. He had soon come to his senses, however, as he had sat underneath the pulpit and heard the voice of Inspector Andreou. In that split second between hearing Andreou's voice and the terrible sound of a truck careering down the street, followed by people outside screaming, Officer Cadet Danny Mills had found that his mind had been made up for him. He had stepped forward and introduced himself. The inspector had told Danny to come with him, that he would make sure he was safe and protected.

As they had walked back down the ancient market street of Kolossi village, Andreou had told Danny Mills that it was probably best for him to avert his gaze from the crowd that had surrounded the eighteen-wheeler truck. Danny had said that he wasn't fazed by grisly sights. Inspector Andreou pushed his way to the front of the crowd, Danny Mills following closely behind.

The first thing he had seen was a collection of body parts. A chunky human ankle still dressed in a mangled sandal lay alone about six feet from the front right wheel of the truck. Half an arm, pale and fat, lay by itself at the opposite side of the road. Danny had felt repulsed and quite disturbed by what he was looking at but had ignored the instinct to look away, feeling somehow intrigued by the sight that he saw. Inspector Andreou tried to herd the spectators away, with assurances that police and paramedics were on their way.

An old man had opened the back of the truck to allow the animals inside to get some flow of air. His good intentions had accidentally made the situation all the more bizarre, as most of the animals inside, predominantly goats, had managed to escape and were now rampaging along the street. Inspector Andreou had watched in a state of bewilderment at the odd spectacle. Crying children, rampaging goats and a collection of human remains all made for an interesting scene. An old woman was comforting the driver of the truck, offering her best assurances that he couldn't possibly have seen the bizarre turn of events coming. Andreou had heard another elderly woman say to a friend that the noise the truck's brakes had made before the incident were enough of a warning in themselves.

'Inspector,' Danny had interrupted, pulling at his left arm. 'I think I know who that is.'

The young soldier was pointing at what was left of the face of the man squashed to death under the truck. 'That's the man that slapped me and Phil around at Sergii's nightclub the other night. He was called Little Sam.'

Inspector Andreou had tried to keep his look of composure. It wasn't easy as Danny's words had just confirmed Andreou's suspicion that Sergii Filatov was somehow involved in what was going on at the British bases.

Shortly afterwards, a number of marked police cars from the local force had arrived at the scene, along with an ambulance and a medical doctor. The doctor had, somewhat bizarrely, been required to confirm that the victim was indeed dead. Several paramedics had scooped up what was left of Little Sam and placed his remains in medical bags. They had been sealed and placed in the back of an ambulance to be driven away to the local hospital for disposal. Andreou had called over a younger officer. He had explained to him that he was busy. Although Danny Mills hadn't been able to understand the conversation they held in Greek, he had heard the words 'Little Sam' being repeated. He had also understood that Inspector Andreou had given his colleague orders to search for a vehicle that might have belonged to Little Sam.

Given the small size of the village and the community that lived there, it hadn't taken the young officer, an enthusiastic Detective Artemis Aristidou, much time to locate the vehicle that Little Sam had driven. One of the locals had told him that a white Audi convertible had been spotted on the outskirts of the village. None of the locals knew who it belonged to. Detective Aristidou stood by the side of the vehicle, running a trace on the registration plates. The name that they were registered to came back as a Mr Sergii Filatov of Nicosia. Aristidou called his colleagues in Nicosia, asking them to inform Mr Filatov that his car had been found abandoned and that they suspected it had been driven by the now-dead Little Sam.

They also informed Sergii Filatov that his vehicle would have to be impounded until further notice as the police may need it as evidence.

'What the hell kind of evidence are you looking for?' Sergii had ranted down the phone. 'Isn't it bad enough that my best friend has been killed? Now you want my car as well?'

If Sergii had stopped to think about what he was saying, he would have realized that he was right. Little Sam had been his best friend and had certainly considered his boss to be his best mate. Sergii, thinking like a typical psychopath, however, was more concerned with what he would do now that Little Sam wasn't around to follow his orders and enforce the kind of discipline at Colours Nightclub that Sergii wanted.

He was also preoccupied by the fact that his car was to be impounded. He tried to think about what may be inside; what contents Little Sam had taken with him. He knew that Little Sam had liked to use cocaine. That was something that he could easily dismiss if the police asked. He could say that it was nothing to do with him. What Sergii didn't realize, however, was that his now-dead friend Little Sam had been careless. Sergii wasn't the kind of man that dwelled on the past. He preferred to think about the future. He had also become comfortable in his position of power and had made mistakes without realizing it, delegating power perhaps a little too much.

The fact that John Riley's dead and

bloodied body had been transported by Little Sam and Stanislav Young in the very same car that the police now held for inspection was not something that Sergii Filatov was at all aware of.

18

Wednesday 22 August, 2.30 p.m.
Episkopi Garrison
Western Sovereign Base Area
Cyprus

Warehouse number five, once used for the storage of military vehicles, had sat empty for several years. Dr Rebekah Terrobias and a team of nurses that worked on the base had been busy setting up a ticket-token system throughout the day, in readiness for collecting urine samples from all military personnel. Each ticket was coded with the military ID of every member of staff. As the designated time approached, a queue of more than five hundred soldiers had already started to line up along the outer walls. A local private hospital in Limassol that went by the name of 'The Polyclinic' had supplied the base with 2,000 small hard plastic cups. They were standard-issue white urine-sample collection kits. A military plane that had flown in during the morning had brought with it a further 5,000 units. They would be distributed evenly across all of the bases that formed the

Sovereign Base Areas. Each looked the same, emblazoned with the name DRUGSMART across the front. Single-use and multi-purpose, each cup had been designed to quickly and efficiently trace samples of cannabis, cocaine, benzodiazepines, amphetamines, methamphetamines and opiates, including heroin. A sticker across the front had to be peeled back after a wait of six minutes following urine collection. A negative result would be indicated by the presence of two red lines under the relative drug name. Cannabis, or THC, for example, if negative, would show itself with the two red lines that all were hoping for. However, a single red line by itself would tell the nurses that the person whose urine was inside the cup had been found to be positive for the substance indicated on the outside. Inside the warehouse, the nurses had established twenty 'testing stations' each manned by two nurses. Forty soldiers or personnel could therefore be tested simultaneously. Each testing station had been fitted with two khaki curtains, to allow privacy. Of the 7,000 military personnel and their families spread across all of the British bases on the island, only the servicemen and women themselves would be subjected to the testing regime. Of these, approximately 2,700 would today gather at warehouse number five.

Dr Terrobias stood at a long trestle table close to the entrance of the warehouse. She was working out how long she could expect her working day to last. *Approximately sixty-seven groups of forty personnel equal 2,700 staff, thereabouts,* she thought to herself. *At the quickest, each group will take five minutes.*

She changed her mind. *No, make that ten minutes to allow for their usual banter and delays. Not everyone pees at the same speed, especially under stress. That means that sixty-seven groups taking ten minutes will take approximately just over eleven hours to complete.*

It would indeed be a long evening ahead that would take Dr Terrobias and her team through to the early hours of the morning. She thought it was kind of Dr Laos to volunteer to help. Not that one extra person would speed things along.

Dr Laos hadn't yet arrived but Rebekah Terrobias decided that it was time to begin the process. She started by asking all of her own staff to do their urine tests as they too were military personnel. She knew that she personally would be able to check the results of the nurses' urine samples in a little under twenty minutes. She would then test herself as required and ask one of the nurses to verify the results.

Each time an individual completed the urine sample analysis, their military personnel identification number would be taken from a large sheet of sticky-backed ID numbers with bar codes and placed onto a separate sheet and the name subsequently removed from the database. She took a pair of sterile examination gloves and waited for the nursing staff to hand them their own test cups. She worked quickly and with each result returned, disposed of the samples in a medical bin that would be incinerated.

Forty nurses down, she thought to herself as she placed the last ID sticker into the results book. *All negative*. She then did her own urine sample under the supervision of one of the nursing staff. *Also negative*. She asked the soldier that stood at the door of the warehouse to do his urine sample. She checked the results.

The forty-second negative.

The front door to the warehouse was opened by the soldier. Dr Terrobias saw the extensive queue formed along the outside walls. It had grown since the last time she checked. She was ready to give the soldier at the door the order to let in the first group of 40 personnel as Dr Laos appeared at the head of the queue.

'Rebekah, how's it going here?' she asked as she walked into the warehouse.

'Well, Dr Laos. All of the nursing staff, myself and the soldier at the entrance are negative.'

Karen winked at her young colleague. 'In that case, let's get the process going, shall we?'

She moved into the warehouse and let the soldier on duty call forward the first group. Forty soldiers walked in. The warehouse took on a new air of activity. Dr Laos found herself admiring the efficiency of the system that had been implemented.

'Tell me, Rebekah, what's the process to be followed should a test result return as positive?'

'Inspector Haws told me not to immediately alert the individual in such a case. He will keep a list of any positive test results and round the individuals up later for blood analysis.'

'That's a good idea,' replied Karen. 'You know that these sample tests are not entirely reliable?'

Rebekah Terrobias thought. 'Well, I know they're not as reliable as a blood-test but they do claim to be 99.9 per cent accurate.'

'Yes,' agreed Dr Laos. 'They are very useful

tools in the detection of illicit substances, but they are certainly not foolproof. One badly manufactured sample cup is bound to be present out of the large number of those we have here.'

She indicated the large boxes along the walls that contained almost 7,000 individual units.

Ten minutes passed and the next group of soldiers was called in. Those that had just finished as part of the first group left the warehouse as noisily as they had come in.

Wednesday 22 August, 3 p.m.
Officer Cadets' Barrack; Block B6
Episkopi Garrison
Western Sovereign Base Area
Cyprus

Block B6 of the Officer Cadets Barrack housed twenty young soldiers at any one time. Each of the ten rooms within had been designed in exactly the same way as the room in which Phil Wakely had taken his own life; the room that he had shared with Danny Mills. That room, number nine, on the top floor, had been released from its earlier status as a crime scene. Police Constable Steve Harrington of the Western Sovereign Base

Area's Military Police Division had worked his way through the first four floors of the barrack and had located nothing suspicious so far. He had been teamed with a policewoman from the Cyprus Joint Police Unit. His dog, which had been appropriately named Action, was a 3-year-old male Labrador. Steve Harrington had worked with Action since he was a puppy. They had formed a unique bond between them. Steve learned as much from his dog as the dog had learned from his handler. Steve's friends often teased him that he and Action were like a married couple. Steve didn't mind. He knew that his colleagues had as much respect for Action as they did for their human counterparts. He had already served a successful year in Afghanistan where he had worked with Steve on detecting roadside explosive devices.

Constable Harrington found it somewhat amusing that the female cop he was with today, a Julia Anastasiou, kept calling Action 'Mr Action'. He hadn't realized until he had asked her why, that it was actually a local and perfectly normal use of the Greek language when translated literally into English. He quickly realized that that had been why the Cypriots he had met had called him Mr Steve. Constable Harrington, Mr Action and

Julia Anastasiou now entered the fifth floor of the barrack.

'Is this the room you told me about, Mr Steve?' asked Anastasiou, pointing to the room that Wakely and Mills had shared.

'Yes, it is. Don't worry. The pathologist and Inspector Haws have cleared the room for inspection. The body was removed several hours ago.'

'Still,' she said, 'it gives me the creeps knowing that someone killed himself in that room.'

'Well,' Steve answered, 'take your pick. We've got two rooms left in this building to check.'

'Let's go into the non-suicide room first, shall we?' pleaded Anastasiou, referring to room number ten.

Harrington smiled at her and opened the door of the room that sat adjacent to the one in which Phil Wakely had killed himself. Mr Action walked in first. He sniffed a great deal around the room, with Steve Harrington encouraging him all the time with verbal praise and food treats.

'Why is he circling like that?' asked Anastasiou.

'That,' said Steve, 'means he thinks he has found something.'

They watched as Mr Action stopped

circling and sat down in front of one of the beds.

'That means he is sure he's found something,' said Steve as he approached Mr Action and rewarded him with a treat.

'Help me out, will you, Julia?' he called as he started lifting the mattress off the bed.

Mr Action wagged his tail. Julia took the other end of the mattress and together they lifted it up and placed it against the wall. Mr Action walked over to the mattress and sniffed in a circular pattern at every inch of it. He then went back on himself and pawed at the centre of the mattress. Steve removed a penknife from his belt and cut a hole in the mattress. He pulled the hole with his fingertips and opened it up. Mr Action again sat down and wagged his tail.

'What do you see?' asked Anastasiou, leaning in to have a look. Steve didn't answer immediately. He turned the mattress on its back.

'There,' he said, pulling the gap wider open. 'In the stitching of the mattress I see a small amount of powder.'

Julia reached at the mattress and pulled the rip wider open. As she tugged at the material, five small bags, each tightly wrapped in plastic material, identical to the ones that had been found in Andrew

Morrison's stomach, fell loose.

'Bingo!' said Harrington, lifting the bags into his hands.

'Our orders are to get anything we find over to warehouse number five so that Dr Laos can take them for forensic analysis.'

He again rewarded Mr Action with a treat. He placed the five small bags into his rucksack and they closed the door shut after them.

'Who lives in this room?' asked Anastasiou.

'I'm afraid I don't know,' replied Harrington. 'Our orders are simply to report all findings to Inspector Haws.'

He lifted his radio from his belt and summoned Chris Haws.

'Sir, this is Constable Harrington. I'm with Officer Anastasiou. We have a positive find to report.'

He waited while Inspector Haws turned his radio to a frequency that would allow only Harrington to hear him.

'What's your location, Constable?' came his reply.

'Room Ten, Block B6 of the Officer Cadets' Barracks, sir.'

'What have you found?' asked the inspector.

'At first guess, I'd say it's cocaine. Action found the substance inside a mattress. In total, there are five small bags.'

'OK, Harrington. Good work. Finish your search of the barrack and get the substances over to Dr Laos at warehouse five.'

'Copy that, sir,' answered Harrington as he switched his radio back to the general frequency they had been instructed to use. They walked out of room number ten and closed the door behind them.

'Now,' said Harrington to Julia Anastasiou. 'Let's get room number nine over and done with, shall we?'

He opened the door. Mr Action walked in first. He again repeated the standard moves that he had been taught when searching for drugs. He sniffed every inch of the room. He stopped by the wardrobe where Phil Wakely had been found dead. This time he did not wag his tail.

'What's he doing now?' asked Anastasiou, still standing near to the entrance of the door.

'He's probably a little confused. He hasn't sat down or wagged his tail, which tells me that he hasn't found any sign of drugs here. However, he is also trained as a search-and-rescue dog. I expect he has picked up on the scent of death.'

'He can do that?' asked Anastasiou. 'Even after all these hours?'

'Oh, yes. He has a far stronger sense of

smell than we really understand. Did you know that dogs can also detect cancer in the human body if properly trained?'

'I had no idea. That must take some clever training.'

Constable Harrington looked at Action as he answered. 'Not really. The dog has all of these skills already preprogrammed into his genetic make-up. We simply bring them out. He does the hard work himself.' He spoke with the voice of a proud parent. Action moved across to the other side of the room, this time circling and wagging his tail.

'Has he found something else?' asked Julia.

'If he has, it's a remnant of a drug that has been in the room, but which was removed, possibly some time ago. We know that Officer Cadet Wakely tested positive for cocaine during the autopsy that Dr Laos performed. It's even possible that Action has picked up on a scent of the drug that Wakely's body excreted.'

He called Action back to him and rewarded him with a treat, before placing him back on his leash.

'We're done here, Julia. Let's get over to the warehouse.'

They left the room and walked down the same flight of stairs that Danny Mills had previously escaped from, and on which Phil

Wakely had ultimately taken his final journey. They exited the building into the strong sunshine.

As they walked away, Air Vice-Marshal Littleton watched from a distance. He took his private mobile phone from his pocket and dialled the same local number with the 99 prefix he had used so often over the years.

'It's me,' he snarled. 'What the hell have you done?'

He heard laughter from the other end.

'I think that's pretty self-explanatory, Littleton. As the note said, we no longer have use for you. We made an executive decision and came to the conclusion that with all this shit going on at the base we're no longer interested in your help.'

'But you need me,' the air vice-marshal spluttered.

'No, we don't. You may need us but we're not going to help you. You can sort your own mess out.'

Littleton had been sweating profusely since the time he had found the drugs in the safe in his office. 'I'm not going down for this. If I go down, I'm taking you with me,' he threatened.

'Good luck with that, David. Look at the bigger picture, will you? You've got an office full of drugs. You've got a murdered soldier,

251

another one that killed himself and of course the unexplained death of John Riley. Let's not forget you've also got a missing cadet on your hands. That's a lot for you to deal with. I'd think you probably wished you were dead yourself by now?'

The voice laughed again.

'I'm not that desperate,' lied the air vice-marshal in his own defence.

'Oh, really? From what I hear you've got nowhere to run. The base has been closed to all military personnel. That includes you. They'll get to you in time, Littleton.'

'I'm still the commanding officer,' shouted the air vice-marshal, barely believing his own words. 'I'm going to speak to Inspector Haws and tell him that Stanislav Young is the killer.'

His contact laughed at him yet again. 'And where do you think Stanislav is?'

It was then in that awful second of realization that it dawned upon David Littleton that Stanislav Young was not a military employee and had therefore more than likely fled the base by now.

'You sick bastard,' he said, feeling the walls close in on him.

'Yep, that I may be, but you knew that from the start. Stanislav is here with me, safely out of your way. In fact, we're enjoying a beer together as we talk.'

As Littleton hung up the call, he heard Stanislav Young shouting 'Hi, David' in the background as he drank with his friend Charlie Charalambos.

19

Inspector Chris Haws pulled his troop-car into a small enclave of bushes on the outer perimeter of the garrison's military personnel exit. He checked his watch and looked around him. He saw a Cyprus Joint Police Unit vehicle driving towards his own car. As the car came closer, he saw Inspector Andreou at the wheel and, in the passenger seat next to him, Officer Cadet Danny Mills. He got out of his car and stood next to the door. Andreou pulled in alongside him. Danny Mills got out first. He walked towards Inspector Haws.

'I'm sorry, sir,' he said. 'I didn't know what to do after Phil killed himself. I was scared and stupid and just ran.'

Dimitris Andreou locked the car as he got out and walked over to the young soldier.

Inspector Haws gave Danny a gentle tap on the shoulder. 'All we're concerned about, Mr

254

Mills, is that you are safe. There will be time later for you to explain yourself. Ultimately you have done the right thing. You turned yourself in and for that I can assure you that your record will be expunged.'

Danny Mills looked grateful.

'I told you, Danny,' said Andreou, 'that you would be fine coming back here.'

'Thanks,' replied Danny.

Inspector Andreou moved in closer to Chris Haws. 'Young Danny has been telling me some very interesting things. From what he says, it is very likely that Phil Wakely killed himself because of an experience they shared in the early hours of Tuesday morning.'

'Tell me about it, Danny,' said Haws, looking back to Danny Mills.

'We were stupid, sir. We wanted to get some justice for Andrew Morrison. He was a mate of ours. We saw him last week at Colours Nightclub in Limassol. He was talking to that Russian guy, Sergii. They seemed to get on quite well but then things changed. I saw Sergii shouting at Andrew but I couldn't hear what was said. The next thing I knew, Andrew had left the club in a rush and was later found dead. Phil and I thought that Sergii and his group were somehow involved so we went back on Monday night to ask him.'

Inspector Haws looked somewhat shocked. 'You went to confront Sergii Filatov?' he asked.

'Yes, sir. Phil and I had a few drinks and we were more confident than realistic after that. But when we got there, Sergii wasn't there. Some guy called Igor took us to see that bloke that got squashed by the truck in Kolossi. They called him Little Sam.'

'Little Sam was known to us for years,' interjected Inspector Andreou. 'He was one of Filatov's most loyal employees. Someone had obviously informed Filatov that we were looking for young Danny here and he sent Little Sam to track us.'

Inspector Haws thought about his colleague's words. 'Well, we have one good thing on our side, in that case. I assume that Little Sam never got the chance to tell Sergii that he had seen you or Danny?'

'I don't see how it would have been possible,' replied Andreou. 'I found Danny in a small church. It seems that Little Sam spotted me and tried to follow me across the road. There was a market on the street. He somehow ended up getting pulled under the eighteen-wheeler as he was crossing the road to find me. I don't think he even had the chance to see Danny at all.'

'Good,' answered Inspector Haws.

He patted Danny on the head. 'That means that as far as Sergii Filatov is concerned, you're still missing. I want it to stay that way.'

'He'll find out though, sir, now I'm back on the base,' replied Danny.

'What makes you say that, Danny?'

'He's got a friend here. A guy called Stanislav. It was him that made sure Phil and I got back into the base yesterday morning. He works at the civilian personnel entrance on the gate. I guess that Sergii called him and told him to make sure we got back in unnoticed.'

Inspector Haws picked up his radio and called the gateman on duty at the civilian entrance.

'This is Inspector Haws. I need to know where Stanislav Young is.'

He waited while the gateman checked his logs.

'Sir, Stanislav Young hasn't been seen since his last shift. He isn't subject to the current curfew as he's not a military employee.'

Shit, the inspector thought to himself.

'OK, noted. Haws out.' He turned to Andreou. 'This might actually work better for us. With Stanislav gone there's nobody that we know of who can inform Sergii Filatov that Danny is back safely.'

He suddenly recalled his conversation

earlier with Dr Karen Laos.

'There is just one other person I don't want to know that you're back yet, Danny,' he said.

'Who is that?' asked Inspector Andreou.

Chris Haws spoke quietly. 'I want what I am about to tell you both to stay between us. I shared some suspicions I have with Dr Laos. Unfortunately my suspicions tell me that Air Vice-Marshal Littleton is somehow involved in all of this.'

Andreou nodded. 'I thought the same, Chris, but I didn't say anything as there's no evidence for such a connection.'

'Wait,' said Danny. 'What makes you think that the air vice-marshal is involved with the likes of Sergii Filatov?'

'Call it a gut feeling, Danny,' replied Inspector Haws. 'It's a gut feeling, I may add, that is shared by both myself and Inspector Andreou as well as Dr Karen Laos.'

'Dr Laos?' Andreou asked. 'What makes Dr Laos think that Littleton is involved?'

'Although I haven't known her very long, I trust her judgment implicitly,' said Haws. 'If you'd seen the way she tackled Littleton the first time she met him, you'd understand what I mean. She pulled him up on several aspects of his command, including the fact that the death of John Riley wasn't properly investigated at the time of his demise. She also questioned other aspects of Littleton's decision-making. She told me that she found him anything other than professional. It got me thinking about my own experiences working with Littleton over the years. I realized that she was spot-on. I recalled all the times that he had hampered my efforts, in various investigations.'

'Where is Littleton now?' Andreou asked.

'As far as I know he's in his office, as he is always. He tried to interfere earlier on today when I was organizing the search teams.'

He looked at Danny Mills. 'I'm not only referring to the search for you, Danny. We have also implemented drug screens on the base today as a result of the autopsies that Dr Laos conducted on both Andrew Morrison and Phil Wakely. Both were found to be positive for cocaine. The cocaine found in their bodies was an exact match — meaning that they got the drug from the same source.'

'Sir,' said Danny, 'there is something else. I also took cocaine on Tuesday morning. I didn't want to, nor did Phil. Sergii Filatov told us that we had to earn what he called 'credit' to cancel out the 'debit' we had created by accusing him of killing Andrew Morrison.'

'What did Filatov tell you would be your

reward?' asked Andreou.

'Our lives,' answered Danny. 'He said that we had a choice. It wasn't much of a choice, though. It was either end up dead like Morrison had, or agree to take the cocaine and encourage our mates to take it as well. He said we were his newest employees and that we should return to Colours Nightclub this weekend with other soldiers and get them to take the drug.'

'That son of a bitch,' said Inspector Haws.

'Employees indeed? That,' said Andreou, 'is how Filatov works. He is a master of manipulation and threatens people into doing things that benefit him. What else did he say, Danny? How did he react when you accused him of killing Lieutenant Morrison?'

'He said that he hadn't killed Morrison but that he knew who had. He said it was the British bases. Phil called him stupid, or something like that, and said he was talking crap when he told us that Morrison was a druggie.'

'I can't imagine that Sergii liked that much,' Inspector Haws said.

'No, he didn't. He punched Phil hard in the stomach,' replied Danny. 'He told us that John Riley had been killed by the British, not him. He said that Morrison had accused him of killing Riley and that he had given

Morrison the same choices he claimed to give us: get involved with the whole drug scene or end up dead. I guess that Andrew was in a tough position and when he decided he'd had enough, he paid the price that Sergii said we would end up paying if we didn't do what he wanted: get killed.'

Inspector Haws addressed Andreou. 'Tell me, Dimitris, how much faith do you place in what Sergii Filatov says?'

The inspector thought for a while. 'Good question, Chris,' he replied. 'Sergii says a lot of stuff; most of it has some truth to it. He is many things but ironically enough, I have never caught him out on a bare-faced lie. If what Danny had told us just now had come from Charlie Charalambos, I wouldn't pay any attention to it. But knowing Filatov as I do, I would have to say that what we've heard is pretty reliable. There may be a few deceptions mixed in, but plain lies? I doubt it.'

'Good,' replied Inspector Haws. 'That means that given what we've heard, we need to make a move somehow.'

'Any ideas?' asked Andreou.

'Actually,' replied Chris Haws, 'I do have one idea.' He turned to Danny Mills. 'Danny, just how far are you willing to go to help us put an end to all this crap that's been going on?'

Danny didn't hesitate in answering. 'Sir, I think after all I've seen over the past few days, I would be prepared to do anything required if it meant you can catch that Sergii guy.'

Inspector Haws grinned broadly. 'In that case, let's get back to my office. I have a suggestion.'

They headed back to their cars.

'Danny, keep your head low on the way in; the fewer people that know you're back, the better,' added Haws.

'Oh, there's something else, Chris,' said Inspector Andreou as he opened his car door. 'We've got Little Sam's car in custody. It's registered to Filatov.'

20

Air Vice-Marshal David Littleton sat at his desk, looking straight at the safety deposit box that had been meant to protect him from taking the fall for everything that he had been involved with. On the desk in front of him sat the bank statements detailing his vast wealth, accrued through criminality and greed. He had tried to close the safety deposit box, but the person who had booby-trapped it had been smart. Once opened, it would not reclose. The thick Perspex teased him as he had tried to remove it.

The drugs within, and the note that told him in no uncertain terms that his luck had run out, seemed to stare back in his direction. He stood up and inserted a CD into his stereo system. He turned the volume up just loud enough for no one else outside of his office to hear. He flicked to track number three, and set the song to repeat mode. The sound of Kirsty MacColl's hauntingly clear voice, singing her rendition of 'Miss Otis Regrets', started to play through the speakers. Littleton returned to his desk. The accompanying bagpipes of the First Battalion of Irish Guards came secondary to Kirsty's emotive vocals.

He reached for his favourite pen and a military issued notepad, which bore his personal seal and title. He started to write, as a few unusual and unexpected tears started to roll down his face.

If I had my time again, there are so many things I would have done differently. If I had the chance to run, I would be long gone. But everything happened so quickly.

He lifted a glass from his desk and filled it with straight whisky. It was poured from a bottle that he had been given by the captain of the now retired luxury liner the *QE2*. He had kept it in his office where it had sat in pride of place since he had arrived in Cyprus to take over the position of commanding officer.

He drank a glassful and returned to his note.

I never wanted this. The circumstances I find myself in are entirely of my own doing. I tried to help a troubled young man. For the record, his name is Charlie Charalambos. He promised me great wealth for my retirement if I helped him and his friends. Now I find myself at the end of a long and, I would like to think, distinguished career. It all went horribly wrong when I was the commanding officer in Beirut. Many people died as a result of my tendency to turn a blind eye. I saw dollar signs and it's only now, with further deaths that I could have prevented, that I see the error of my ways.

David Littleton reached again for his bottle of QE2 whisky and poured another glass. He threw it down his throat, trying to pluck up some courage.

For the record, I do not know how many young officers have been infiltrated by Charalambos. All I know is that there will undoubtedly be a high number that test positive for cocaine. Treat them fairly and make sure they get the medical help needed to recover. I instruct and request from my superiors at the Ministry of Defence to use the money I appropriated to fund any treatment needed.

He wiped away a stream of tears. A couple of drops fell onto his notepad.

If you find Charalambos, you will find Sergii Filatov. You also need to look for a civilian employee called Stanislav Young. It *was he who killed Andrew Morrison. I should have come forward before now. But I refuse to spend the rest of my days rotting away in a prison cell. I'm going out in my own way. This is my choice.*

He signed his name underneath the note and left it on his desk. He opened a drawer and took out his Heckler & Koch MP5 semi-automatic weapon.

As the field officer took a final sip from his special whisky, he aimed the gun directly into his mouth and pulled the trigger. His head exploded from the back outwards, his skull absorbing the force of the gunshot. His arms dropped either side of his chair and his Heckler & Koch MP5 semi-automatic gun fell with a crash to the floor. Several splashes of blood and brain fell onto the note that the field officer had written, one somewhat ironically right underneath where he had seconds ago signed his name.

Kirsty MacColl continued to sing through the sound of the air vice-marshal's gunshot. The song, still on repeat, rang out over the noise of his death.

21

Wednesday 22 August, 4.50 p.m.
Warehouse No. 5
Episkopi Garrison
Western Sovereign Base Area
Cyprus

Two hours had passed since the start of the drug-screening process. Twelve groups out of the total number of sixty-seven had passed through warehouse number five. Almost 500 military personnel had been tested. Dr Karen Laos approached Rebekah Terrobias, who was busy studying a pile of paperwork in front of her.

'How is everything, Rebekah?' she asked.

Dr Terrobias looked tired. 'Given that there's another nine hours or so ahead of us, not too bad.' She smiled.

'You look tired, Rebekah,' Karen said.

'I am. But there's very little I can do about that, Dr Laos.'

Karen understood her position. She herself was considered the queen of long shifts back at the mortuary over which she presided in Manchester.

'How many positive results have been returned so far?' asked Dr Laos, pulling a chair up to where Rebekah sat.

'Twenty-six personnel have tested positive for cocaine and a further four for cannabis,' she replied.

'So,' Karen responded. 'Out of 500, we have thirty positives. If the trend continues at this rate, we'll be looking at approximately 360 military personnel testing positive for illicit drugs. That's a shockingly high number.'

'I know, I was just doing the maths myself. It makes for depressing reading.'

'Indeed it does,' agreed Dr Laos. 'If you multiply that number by the approximate street value of, for example, cocaine, the picture is all the more bleak. Somebody has made a lot of money from the staff stationed here on the base. On the other hand, if you want to look at the positive side of the situation, if this trend continues, we are looking at approximately 90 per cent of military employees that are not positive for drugs.'

'I hadn't thought of it like that,' Rebekah replied.

'Of course,' continued Karen, 'we have no idea about the other Sovereign Base Areas or how their results will come back.'

'Have you had the chance yet to leave the base, Dr Laos?'

'No, Rebekah, I haven't. It's been one thing after the other since the moment I touched down. Inspector Andreou did say in passing that he would take me out to see the island. I'm still hoping that there's time for that.'

'How long will you be here for?' asked Dr Terrobias.

'I haven't got a clue about that. The Foreign Office and the Ministry of Defence simply said it would be a secondment from my usual duties in Manchester. I suppose I will stay here until my usefulness is deemed to be over.'

'Would you stay, if you had the chance to?' enquired Dr Terrobias.

'You mean permanently?'

'Yes, if the MOD offered you a full-time position.'

'I don't think so, Rebekah. As much as I love waking up and seeing a blue sky and sunshine every day, I have responsibilities back home. Why do you ask?'

'I'm just curious. It seems to me that we could do with a professional like you being around. I mean, you're not just a pathologist. You're a forensic pathologist. That means you have an inherent knack for seeing past the obvious and looking for clues that the rest of us miss.'

'That's very kind of you to say so, Rebekah,

but not entirely true. You're doing a great job here. I was very impressed by your skills when we worked together on the autopsies.'

Karen's praise suddenly made Rebekah feel more awake than she had previously.

'Thanks, Dr Laos. That means a lot to me. I still have a lot to learn, though.'

'From what I've seen, you'll excel in whichever area of medicine you might decide to follow further.'

The young soldier who had been standing guard at the entrance to the warehouse approached.

'Dr Laos,' he said. 'Excuse me for interrupting but I've just had a call from Inspector Haws. He is asking that you go to his office.'

Karen looked at Rebekah. 'Will you be OK here, Dr Terrobias?'

'Yes, Dr Laos, I'll be fine. Thank you.'

'OK, I'll come back to see you as soon as possible.'

Karen Laos gathered her belongings and walked out of the warehouse. Several soldiers who were lined up outside stopped talking as she passed them by. Dr Laos had the distinct feeling that she was being talked about.

There she goes. The interfering doctor that brought this upon us all.

She brushed her suspicions aside and continued onward to Inspector Haws' office.

Wednesday 22 August, 5:10 p.m.
Office of Inspector Chris Haws
Sovereign Base Areas Police Headquarters
Episkopi Garrison
Western Sovereign Base Area
Cyprus

Dr Laos arrived at Inspector Haws' office and found the inspector, Danny Mills and Inspector Dimitris Andreou waiting for her. Inspector Haws beckoned to her to take a seat. He duly took a large jug of water and poured four glasses.

'Dr Laos,' he started. 'Thanks for coming.'

Karen looked at Danny Mills. 'I assume you're Mr Mills?' she asked, her hand extended in greeting.

'Yes,' he replied, reciprocating her gesture.

'Dr Laos, I have asked you to come here for several reasons,' said Haws. 'I have discovered the benefit over the past few days in working closely with you. I have been telling my guests the same thing.'

Inspector Andreou nodded his confirmation.

'Danny has been filling us in with regard to

271

the events that led to his fleeing from the base on Tuesday afternoon. By all accounts, he has had quite a time of it. Danny has also confirmed that on Monday night, he and Phil Wakely went to Limassol to speak to Sergii Filatov. They had seen Filatov speaking to Andrew Morrison shortly before his death on Saturday morning. He admits that he made a mistake in returning to Filatov's Colours Nightclub but says that both he and Mr Wakely thought they could get some justice for their dead friend, Andrew.'

Karen looked at Danny Mills. 'That was an admirable sentiment, Danny, but one that could have seen you end up in the same way that Andrew did,' she said.

'I know,' replied Danny. 'It was stupid.'

'The long and short of it, Dr Laos, is that when Danny and Phil arrived at the night-club, they were taken hostage by Filatov's thug, the now-deceased Little Sam. He gave them a hard time,' said Inspector Haws.

'I understand,' replied Dr Laos. 'What did they do to you, Danny?'

'Little Sam's boss arrived and gave us an ultimatum. He said that we had offended him by accusing him of killing Andrew. He said that we could repay the debt by working for him. He made us take cocaine and told us that we were to return to his club this weekend with some other soldiers from the base. Detective Haws thinks that Sergii has plans to recruit more soldiers in the same way he did with Phil and me.'

'That makes sense,' answered Karen, 'given all I have heard about this Sergii Filatov. Did he mention Charlie Charalambos to you?'

'No, but both Inspector Haws and Inspector Andreou are working on that.'

Inspector Andreou leaned in towards Dr Laos. 'Dr Laos, given what Danny has told us about his taking cocaine when he was at Colours Nightclub, is there any way that you can test Danny and confirm that the cocaine is from the same source as that found in Andrew Morrison and Mr Wakely?'

'Of course, Inspector. Our early studies of the substance found in Andrew Morrison's body were quite revealing, namely the fact that it could only have originated in Peru. Add to that the fact that we know it was of a purity of 97 per cent, which is extremely unusual, I would be quite confident in running a comparison.'

She looked at Danny Mills. 'Danny, that is of course given that you would be willing for me to take a blood sample from you?'

'I've got no problem with that, Dr Laos. I was telling the inspectors that I would be willing to do anything to help now.'

'Great,' replied Dr Laos. She reached for her bag and took out a needle, syringe, blood-specimen tube and a tourniquet. 'Danny, this won't hurt a bit. Believe me I have done this thousands of times.'

Danny extended his left arm out flat and made a fist. Karen prepped his median cubital vein, which ran along the inner part of his forearm, and quickly inserted the needle. She collected one tube of blood and concluded the procedure by placing a small plaster on the spot from which she had drawn blood.

'I will have the results ready this evening,' she promised, as she put the specimen inside her bag.

'Great, thank you Dr Laos,' said Inspector Andreou.

Karen was ready to reply to Dimitris Andreou, when Inspector Haws' telephone started ringing. The look on his face when he answered had Dr Laos, Danny Mills and Inspector Andreou on tenterhooks.

'I understand,' he said. 'When did this happen?' His face had turned a ghostly shade of grey. He ended the call and addressed his guests.

'The air vice-marshal is dead. His secretary just found him in his office. It seems that he killed himself.'

Nobody spoke, but each mirrored the other as they collected their belongings and stood up. Inspector Haws looked at Danny Mills.

'Danny, I don't know whether your coming is such a good idea. You've already seen one suicide in the past couple of days. I'm not sure that it would be wise for you to witness another one.' He looked at Inspector Andreou.

'Quite right. I agree with Inspector Haws,' he said, having picked up on his colleague's facial expression. 'I will stay here with Danny and wait for you to return.'

Dr Laos and Inspector Haws left the office and walked in silence to where they would start investigating the death of Air-Vice Marshal David Littleton, leaving Danny Mills once more in the company of Inspector Andreou.

Wednesday 22 August, 6 p.m.
Forensic Science Directorate
Limassol Central Police Headquarters
Limassol
Cyprus

Detective Artemis Aristidou had been due to sign off his day shift at 4 p.m. He had promised his wife and kids that he would take them out this evening. It had been a long time since he had dedicated some proper time to his family. However, the excitement had soon grown throughout the local police force when word had spread that one of Sergii Filatov's boys had been killed. The fact that they had one of Sergii's cars in their custody had been a talking point among the officers all afternoon. The normally sedate team at the forensic science division had all been more than willing to put in some extra overtime if it meant that they had a better chance of finally finding something that could be used to apprehend Filatov.

The white Audi convertible that Little Sam had driven now sat on a raised platform in their care. Detective Aristidou had been instructed by Inspector Andreou to oversee the operation by the forensic scientists and to make sure that the vehicle was searched from top to bottom. Mechanics had started to strip the car down, piece by piece. The scientists worked in pairs, each carefully analyzing every inch of the car parts that they were given. On face value, the car was clean and had been maintained in immaculate condition. The car insurance, road tax and MOT were fully up to date and all of the paperwork associated with the car appeared to be in good order. Aristidou knew, however, that if they were to find any trace of anything incriminating, the car would have to be subjected to a thorough forensic sweep. One of his colleagues had been excited to see several spots of what he thought to be dried blood on the back seats of the car. Aristidou had told him that you can't just assume that everything you see is a sign of something more sinister. The red spots on the back seats had turned out to be nothing more than discolouration from the sun.

One of the forensic scientists was busy subjecting the vehicle's upholstery to luminol testing. This was the chemical process that the scientists used in order to try to reach some meaningful conclusions. The luminol chemiluminescence reaction that they now used was the same effect that had been produced in the glow of light-sticks, commonly seen in nightclubs. In this test, the scientists mixed luminol powder with hydrogen into a spray bottle specially adapted for their investigative purposes.

One of the scientists, Maria Papagalos, was carefully spraying the solution across all areas of fabric within the vehicle. A crime-scene photographer followed her every movement. If any traces of blood were found on the upholstery of the vehicle, the chemical reaction would produce a blue glow that would last no longer than thirty seconds. This thirty-second window would give the photographer the time needed to take images of the glowing reaction.

The iron from the haemoglobin in any blood that had been left in the vehicle would serve as a catalyst for the chemiluminescence reaction that causes luminol to glow. Even the tiniest amount of iron from blood that had been cleaned would be enough to cause the chemical reaction to give a positive result. As Maria sprayed, she waited patiently for any signs of a reaction. She sprayed the front seats first, and the carpet underneath. It wasn't until she reached the rear of the vehicle that she called out in excitement.

'Detective!' she shouted. 'We've got ourselves a trace of blood on the carpet underneath the driver and passenger seats.'

Aristidou moved in close enough to see the distinctive blue glow. The photographer took several shots. Papagalos continued to spray the solution, this time working up from the floor of the car. After a few more sprays of the solution, she again called out 'Positive!'

The photographer flashed again on his camera. Papagalos took a small test tube for collection. Although there was nothing visible to the naked eye, she now knew where to remove the blood traces. With the help of a metallic scraper, she lifted the invisible blood from the upholstery and placed it in the test tube. She got out of the vehicle and moved to a chemical workstation. She took a small solution of potassium ferricyanide and added a drop of industrial-strength alcohol. She passed the test tube to Detective Aristidou.

'Make sure that this gets to Inspector Andreou, will you?' she asked.

'That's exactly what I intend to do,' he replied. 'He's at the British base. Although we don't have the facilities here to run this blood sample against any known missing or murder cases, the inspector tells me that there is one unsolved case that is of particular interest to the British. They've drafted in the help of a forensic pathologist, Dr Karen Laos. She can run a comparison on the sample you've managed to find with the blood record they have on file of the case they want to solve.'

He walked away.

'Call me if you find anything else,' he shouted as he made his way to his car.

22

Wednesday 22 August, 6.30 p.m.
Central Command
Episkopi Garrison
Western Sovereign Base Area
Cyprus

Air Vice-Marshal Littleton's secretary sat on a chair in the corridor adjacent to the office in which his lifeless corpse now sat. She sobbed more from shock than any great sense of loss. Dr Laos and Inspector Haws were inside the office.

'Interesting choice of exit music,' said Dr Laos as she turned off the air vice-marshal's stereo and stopped Kirsty MacColl in the middle of the chorus.

'Exit music?' asked Inspector Haws.

'Yes, you know. The song choice that people make when they kill themselves.'

'The smell is awful,' said the detective.

'I'm afraid that's the smell of suicide by a fatal gunshot wound,' replied Dr Laos. She handed him a tub of what was affectionately called 'Y-cream' and told him to apply a layer of it under his nostrils. He looked at the tub.

'But that's nothing more than Vick's VapoRub,' he said as he looked at the tub.

'I know,' Karen replied. 'We call it Y-cream in reference to the Y-shaped incision we make during most autopsies.'

Inspector Haws applied it as instructed. 'Don't you need some, Dr Laos?' he asked.

She smiled at him. 'No, Inspector. Let's just say my nostrils have grown accustomed to foul smells.' She moved towards the body. In her hands, she carried a Panasonic wide-angle-lens camera, equipped with a variety of millimetre options for different photograph modes. She also had a Dictaphone in her pocket. She reached for it and turned it on. She started to describe the room in detail.

'What are you doing?' asked Inspector Haws.

'I'm following procedure, Inspector. It's important that all crime scenes are fully documented for legal reasons.'

'But you didn't do that this morning when Phil Wakely's body was found.'

'I didn't, but the officers that were present were instructed to. Besides, this is a far more messy and complex scenario.'

She continued speaking into her Dictaphone. 'The deceased appears at first sight to have died as a result of a gunshot wound which, given the appearance of the victim's body position and head, suggests that it was a self-inflicted traumatic injury. The back of the victim's head has been displaced. This is also consistent with death by a gunshot that was aimed directly into the victim's mouth. The weapon that was apparently used is lying on the floor to the side of the victim's body, suggesting that it fell there after detonation.'

She continued to take photographs of the room and of Littleton's body.

'This is interesting, Inspector,' she called.

Inspector Haws walked over to where Karen stood. 'What's interesting, Dr Laos?'

Karen pointed to the note that the air vice-marshal had written before he had killed himself.

'I would say that's a suicide note.'

She handed Inspector Haws a pair of sterile gloves and a small evidence bag. He put the gloves on and lifted the note from the table.

'My God,' he exclaimed.

'What is it, Inspector?' asked Dr Laos, busily taking photographs of what remained of David Littleton's head.

'This note appears to be a confession. He has named Charlie Charalambos. He also expresses his regret at not having put a stop to things here sooner.'

'Well, in my view that's a little too late,'

282

said Dr Laos, somewhat unsympathetically.

Inspector Haws continued studying the note. 'He also says that the person that killed Andrew Morrison is Stanislav Young, who we know is long gone by now. I asked where he was earlier today when Danny Mills told me that Stanislav had let him and Phil Wakely back into the base the other morning. The air vice-marshal also says that if we find Charalambos we will find Stanislav.'

He radioed through to his colleagues in Central Command, setting his radio to a frequency that he knew Inspector Andreou would be able to hear.

'This is Inspector Haws. Coordinate with the local police and apprehend Charlie Charalambos.'

His colleagues confirmed that they understood a few seconds later. His radio came to life again as Inspector Andreou called him.

'Chris, what's going on?'

'Air Vice-Marshal Littleton left a very telling suicide note in which he names Charlie Charalambos and Stanislav Young. He claims that it was Young that killed Andrew Morrison. I need you to get your colleagues over to Charalambos and take him in. You should find Mr Young with him too.'

'Understood. Did he name Sergii Filatov at all?' asked Andreou.

'No, not directly but I've got a feeling that all of this is coming together and that, as part of that process, we will also be able to apprehend Filatov.'

'You may well be right, Chris. I've just had a message from my colleagues in Limassol. The car that was impounded following Little Sam's death has been searched.'

'What did they find?' asked Haws.

'Blood. A sample of it is being delivered to me by one of my detectives as we speak. Is Dr Laos there with you?'

'I hear you, Inspector!' shouted Karen.

'Dr Laos, I will need to ask you to run an analysis on the sample that's coming in.'

'Of course, Inspector. Just make sure it's left on my desk in the SBA Medical Facility Clinical Laboratory and I will get to it as soon as possible.'

'Understood. Andreou out.'

'Inspector, come here, will you?' asked Dr Laos. 'Do you think this is why the air vice-marshal decided to kill himself?' She was kneeling down next to the safety deposit box.

'It certainly looks as if it would have been a major factor,' replied Inspector Haws. 'A threatening note telling the air vice-marshal that he is no longer required.'

He touched the Perspex cover. 'A seemingly impenetrable layer, and behind it what

284

appears to be bags of cocaine. I'd say it might have been enough for Littleton to realize that his time was running out.'

'My thoughts exactly,' agreed Dr Laos. 'I'll need that Perspex removed and the contents inside delivered to the laboratory as well.'

'You've got a long night ahead of you, Dr Laos.'

'So have you, Inspector,' she replied as she took photographs of the safety deposit box. 'Tell me, Inspector Haws. Who is officially in command of the garrison now that the air vice-marshal is dead?'

'Ordinarily it would be the next highest-ranking officer.'

'And who is that?'

'Right now, the only person on the base that could temporarily step into those shoes would be Major General Morrison.'

'Andrew's father?'

The inspector looked grim. 'I know it's not ideal, but as a temporary measure it's either the major general or the MOD will have to convene military law on the base, which would mean that either I would take temporary command or they will fly someone in from London. The alternating commander from the British Army has been on extended leave for several months. I understand he has been unwell and there's no indication of when he will be returning.'

Karen thought about his words. 'I think it might actually be quite fitting for the major general to take over, given all that's happened; and of course the death of his son. But isn't he retired?'

'Yes, he is. But the MOD could still give him back his rank in a kind of ceremonial role that would oversee Littleton's position until a new replacement is found. I'll make a call to London and see what they think before I ask the major general myself. In the meantime I'm going to head back to my office. I need to speak to Danny Mills and Inspector Andreou.'

'I'll come with you,' said Dr Laos.

She called in a couple of orderlies and gave them instructions to have the air vice-marshal's dead body removed to the mortuary. Inspector Andreou called for a colleague to come and seal off the room and keep the area guarded until further notice. They left the air vice-marshal's office together, leaving Littleton's body in the place he had chosen to kill himself.

'Have you heard from Dr Terrobias at all?' asked Inspector Haws, as they walked back through the adjoining corridor outside.

'No, I haven't. But then, I know she is extremely busy. I'll check in with her later,'

Karen assured the inspector.

Inspector Haws paused as they reached the end of the corridor. 'Actually, Karen,' he said, 'you head to my office. I think I need to speak to Major General Morrison in person and see if he accepts my plan. If he does, I'll then call the MOD.'

Wednesday 22 August, 7 p.m.
No 34, Domnitsas Street
Kallepia
Paphos
Cyprus

Detective Andreas Ioannou had answered the call from Inspector Andreou with great excitement. He had worked quickly to form a SWAT team that would descend upon Charlie Charalambos' house. He picked his best officers for the job and ensured that all were carrying firearms and riot shields. He had apprehended Charalambos in the past and knew that he was a man who would fight back. Ioannou didn't intend to give Charlie the chance to cause any injury to his officers on this occasion.

This was the moment that he and his colleagues had been waiting for, for years. Andreou had told him about the link they had formed between the death of Air Vice-Marshal Littleton, the murder of Andrew Morrison and the additional offence they could arrest Charalambos on: suspicion of supplying Class A drugs.

Detective Ioannou therefore had exactly what he needed. He planned to make two arrests this evening. He had been told that he would find Stanislav Young with Charlie Charalambos. He planned to arrest Stanislav Young on suspicion of the murder of Lieutenant Andrew Morrison. He also planned to arrest Young on the further charge of conspiracy to aid and abet in the supply of Class A drugs. He knew that the latter of the two charges would be the lesser offence but he would deal with that once Stanislav Young was in custody.

When it came to Charalambos, he would arrest him on the primary offence of the supply of Class A drugs. The air vice-marshal's note had also suggested that Charalambos had been involved in the misappropriation of money; that would be his secondary charge. The third would consist of bribery and intimidation.

Detective Ioannou knew that the charges on which he planned to make the arrests were complicated. He wanted, however, to make sure there was enough material to hold

Charalambos on, even if it meant that some of it would be thrown out in a court of law at a later stage.

Ioannou followed a fleet of three police cars and two vans that would act as temporary prisons upon the arrest of Charalambos and Young; his own car was unmarked. The armada came to a stop at the end of Domnitsas Street, twenty metres from Charlie's house.

The street was quiet and deserted. A few lights flickered from the windows of houses number 32 and 33, as Ioannou led his team of ten officers along the pavement that led to Charlie's house. It was difficult to see any sign of activity coming from behind the walled enclosure. Ioannou ordered two of his armed officers to scale the walls, mindful of the position in which Charalambos had set his CCTV cameras.

The first officer reached the top and had a clear line of sight into the kitchen inside. He saw Rafaela preparing a meal at the oven. The second officer indicated to Ioannou that he had a clear line of sight on Charalambos, sitting in front of the television, drinking.

'How many individuals do you see?' asked Ioannou on his radio.

The first officer replied, 'One female in the kitchen in the east wing of the property.'

Ioannou told him to descend into the garden.

The second officer replied, 'I see Charalambos but there's no sign of Stanislav Young.'

Ioannou ordered the second officer into the grounds of the house. He told them both to secure the front and back exits in turn. He sent a further three officers over the wall and told them to get confirmation that Young was inside. He waited two minutes before one of them radioed him back.

'I see Young. He has approached Charalambos.'

Detective Ioannou told two more officers to follow him over the wall. He left the remaining three outside the gates of the house. He told them to ring the bell of the house on his command. He made it over the wall and located the rest of his team. He radioed back to the officers outside and told them to ring the house-bell. A shrill sound rang out from the quietness of the street. It rang again.

'The female is moving to the entrance hallway,' said officer number one. 'Hello, who is it?' she asked, her voice audible over the wall to where Ioannou stood.

'Ma'am, this is the police. We need to speak to Charlie Charalambos.'

The first officer watched as Rafaela called

to Charlie. He appeared in the hallway.

'Charlie's not here, officer,' she lied, unaware that she and her boyfriend were being watched.

Ioannou gave the order for five of the seven officers inside the perimeter of the house to congregate at the front door of the house. He stepped in and banged hard on the wall. He told the five officers to have their weapons ready. They all pulled up their riot shields.

'Charlie, this is Detective Ioannou. I know you're in there. We can see you. Your house is surrounded. Come out peacefully.'

He watched as Charlie approached the front door, a gun in his hands. Charlie opened the door quickly and aimed directly at Ioannou.

'Detective,' he said. 'It's been a long time.'

'Not really, Charlie. I saw you at Zygi's Taverna only yesterday lunchtime.'

Charalambos looked at the large group of officers in front of him.

'No, Charlie, don't!' screamed Rafaela as her boyfriend started firing and rushed towards Ioannou. His bullets bounced off the riot shields, the quietness and stillness of the night replaced by the sound of violence.

Detective Ioannou aimed his gun directly at Charalambos as his colleagues pushed him to the floor, their riot shields squashing his face hard against the concrete of the porch. Charlie reached out and managed to get one more shot at Ioannou. Ioannou felt agonizing pain in his lower left leg as a stray bullet found its way through the group of officers and hit him. It tore through his ligaments and muscle painfully and exited the other side.

As Ioannou fell to the floor in pain, he aimed one single shot at Charlie's head and put him permanently out of action.

Stanislav Young had watched the action unfold and ran to the back door of the house. He saw an officer standing there waiting for him. He backed up on himself and entered a lower-ground guest bedroom. He found a window leading onto the garden. He checked carefully but didn't see any police. He opened the window upwards and tried to snake his way out, the front half of his body getting stuck as the window crashed back down on his abdomen. He yelled out in pain.

The officer at the back door heard his scream and ran to the window of the back bedroom. The officer pushed Young through to the grass beneath.

He pushed hard on Stanislav with his riot shield and cuffed him. As Stanislav Young was dragged around to the front of the house by the burly officer, he saw Charlie lying dead on the porch, Rafaela in handcuffs and Detective Ioannou being tended to by his colleagues. The sound of an ambulance's sirens cried out into the night as it entered Domnitsas Street.

Wednesday 22 August, 8.10 p.m.
Office of Inspector Chris Haws
Sovereign Base Areas Police Headquarters
Episkopi Garrison
Western Sovereign Base Area
Cyprus

Inspector Chris Haws entered his office a little over fifteen minutes later than Dr Laos had returned. His meeting with the major general had been brief and straight to the point. The major general had said that it would be his honour to take over the air vice-marshal's position on a temporary basis until the MOD could locate a permanent replacement. He had also been saddened to hear of Littleton's death, whilst angry and confused over the role that the man he thought was his friend had apparently played in the death of his son, Andrew.

He told Inspector Haws that he would stay as long as needed in order to help 'clean the place up' in service 'of honouring the memory of Andrew and others that have died as a result of David Littleton's corrupt abuse of power'.

Inspector Haws felt quite pleased that he had given the retiree another shot at things. Reinstating the major general on a temporary basis was an easy job for MOD. He would simply oversee the general operations of the base until such a time that a replacement could be found. His role would be largely ceremonial, although the major general had given the impression that he intended to involve himself fully with every aspect of the day-to-day running of the base. He had even told the inspector that he would head over to warehouse number five to assist Dr Terrobias and ensure that the soldiers being tested were 'staying in line'.

Inspector Haws concluded that it was probably better than leaving the old man by himself with his grief. His wife had even seemed excited at the prospect of being the 'first lady'.

'It's not often that one gets another shot at a dream position like this,' the major general had assured his wife.

Major General Morrison understood that all activities currently being undertaken on the base would be left primarily in the hands of Inspector Haws. Still, his enthusiasm for the role wasn't dimmed in the slightest. The inspector arrived back at his office with a renewed sense of purpose.

'Danny, I have a plan that I need to discuss with you,' he said, looking the young man directly in the face. 'I need you to tell me whether you have any doubts about it whatsoever. If you do, we will think of another plan of action.'

Karen knew what was coming, as Inspector Haws had briefly filled her in on his ideas about how to capture Sergii Filatov. She had her doubts about the safety of the operation he proposed, but was also of the opinion that Danny Mills was actually a fine young man, despite the troubles he had got himself into.

'I'm listening, Inspector,' replied Danny.

'OK, Danny, as far as we know, Sergii Filatov has no clue that you are back here on the base with us. Nor does he know that you have told us everything that happened to you the other night. My idea is that you return as planned to Colours Nightclub, preferably tonight, claiming that you had nowhere else to run.'

Inspector Andreou raised an eyebrow. His concern wasn't lost on Inspector Haws, but he continued regardless.

'We will of course be with you all the time. I want Inspector Andreou, under his authority as a police officer of the Republic of

Cyprus, to post his own officers around the building of Colours Nightclub. I will provide some undercover cops to join you. You can claim they are the young soldiers that Filatov asked for. If he asks you how you recruited them so quickly, tell him that they are your closest friends and you called them when you were running and that they agreed to meet you at the club. We will of course make sure that you're wearing a wire, so we can communicate with you at all times; and you with us, should you need to. As soon as we hear something definitive from Filatov, we will be in that building with you immediately. Do you have any questions?'

Danny digested what the inspector had told him. 'Will I be safe?' he asked.

Inspector Haws looked intently at Danny's concerned face.

'I will personally make sure you're safe, Danny. At the first sign of trouble, we will pull you out of there without hesitation. Remember that you won't be alone. The police officers that will pose as your friends are more than able to protect you in case anything goes wrong.'

Inspector Andreou stood up.

'What's on your mind, Dimitris?' asked Chris Haws.

'I'm just thinking about how best to do

this. It's not a problem to get my own officers arranged.'

He took a dry-marker pen from Haws' desk and walked to a whiteboard affixed to the wall.

'Here,' he said, 'is the approximate location of Colours Nightclub.' He sketched a square building at the corner of a long street. On the street he wrote the name, Makarios Avenue. His pen continued moving from east to west.

'The road runs through Limassol's town centre. Here, where I marked the location of Colours Nightclub, there is an intersection. It runs to the north of the city from the left side of the nightclub and down to the Old Town in the south.'

He drew a square to indicate the intersection.

'On the south side heading to the Old Town, there is an abandoned house on the right side of the intersection. Opposite that, on the left side, is a DIY store. Moving back to the same side of the road as Colours Nightclub, there is an arts and craft framing store that takes up the entire corner of the north side of the intersection.' He continued to sketch the locality as he spoke. 'I intend to position armed officers on each corner of the intersection, both at ground level and on the roofs of the buildings. I also plan to plant officers at the back side of the club, where there is a large car park.' He turned to Inspector Haws. 'Chris, how many officers are you planning to send?'

'Well, my officers will have no legal jurisdiction once they are outside of the Sovereign Base's area. They will, however, work closely with you and your team and provide any assistance necessary. To that end, I expect that their support will be better placed inside the nightclub, with Danny. I will send six officers. Three of them will be assigned as Danny's 'friends'. The remaining three will be stationed inside the club and attend under the guise of being club-goers on holiday.'

'Agreed,' replied Inspector Andreou. 'Knowing Sergii Filatov, he won't arrive at the club until at least 2 a.m. He tends to go at the end of the night to collect his money. It's what drives him.'

'In that case, we have plenty of time to make arrangements,' replied Inspector Haws.

23

Wednesday 22 August, 9.30 p.m.
S.B.A Medical Facility — Clinical Labora-tory
Episkopi Garrison
Western Sovereign Base Area
Cyprus

The night was still and the heat stifling, as Karen Laos worked on the increasingly large workload that she had to get through. She had turned the air-conditioning unit on in the laboratory but it seemed to have little effect against the thickness of the humidity; its aging components were fighting a battle that they would inevitably lose. She had instructed the orderlies to place what remained of Air Vice-Marshal Littleton's body into the refrigerated conveyor tray system.

I'll get to him later, she had thought, prioritizing Danny Mill's blood-test results and the analysis of the cocaine that had been found in Littleton's safe. She knew that in terms of investigation, she had to firstly confirm the drug's origin so that the police and eventually the courts would have more in their arsenal to use in the potential prosecution of Sergii Filatov.

A young police officer from Limassol had knocked on the door of Dr Laos' laboratory and, after briefly introducing himself as Detective Artemis Aristidou, had handed her a test tube that he had said contained a blood sample that had been found on the upholstery in the car that Little Sam had driven. He also gave Dr Laos some of the photographs that the photographer who had worked with Maria Papagalos had taken of the car's interior where the luminal chemiluminescence reaction had identified the remains of blood.

Dr Laos thanked the young detective and sent him on his way. She sensed that he was keen to stay to find out the results, but she knew that she had much work to complete and really didn't need distractions. She had listened with interest, however, when he had informed her about the death of Charlie Charalambos.

Word does indeed spread quickly on this small island, she had thought. Artemis had spoken loudly and with excitement as he had regaled Dr Laos with the details of how Charalambos had been killed by his colleagues in Paphos. Karen had felt like she should give the officer her congratulations, so pleased he had seemed to be at the news; but had quickly realized that it would be inappropriate.

She had already conducted her analysis of the blood sample that she had taken from Danny Mills. She sat at her increasingly less-than-temporary desk and studied the results on the print-out that the PE-6800 blood analysis system had produced. Officer Cadet Mills appeared to be a perfectly healthy young man. Dr Laos had performed not only a drug-detection analysis, but had run a standard set of tests, also known as a full blood count, in order to check his general health. Red blood cells, haemoglobin, white bloodcells, lymphocytes and platelets all checked out as within normal ranges. Creatine, urea and glucose also all fell within normal ranges. There were no signs of elevated CPK, which would have indicated infection.

Cocaine results were as expected when exposed to the same SNIF-NMR, Bruker AM-500 machine that had been used previously. The test had only been run in order to again confirm the link between the cocaine that had already been discovered in the dead bodies of Andrew Morrison and Phil Wakely. Danny Mills had already admitted to taking the drug under duress. Karen had started to suspect strongly by now that all of the cocaine that had been found would link back to the same source, including that which had been concealed in Air Vice-Marshal David Littleton's safety deposit box, and of course the numerous urine tests that were coming back from military personnel as positive.

The blood sample that Danny Mills had provided confirmed that the cocaine he had taken when last at Colours Nightclub was of a purity of 97 per cent of the drug's base compound; the exact same result that Dr Terrobias had found when analyzing the drugs that had been located in Andrew Morrison's stomach. Dr Laos moved quickly to the bags of cocaine that had been found in Littleton's safety deposit box. She subjected them to the same steps and procedures that Rebekah Terrobias had with the cocaine found wrapped in bags in Andrew Morrison's stomach. She waited whilst the technology ran various tests, stepping in when needed, applying, for example the Walter's 991 Photodiode Array Detector at the right time.

Results came back within an expected time frame. Again, the drug was found to be of a purity of 97 per cent. Karen made notes as she worked, which she knew would be needed and required by the police for their ongoing investigations; tracing the drugs that had been found to the location of the island where they were being stored, for example; following that hunt, further afield and possibly back to Peru. Although Karen suspected that the local police would simply be pleased enough to get a result in cutting out the local steps of the supply chain.

She typed John Riley's military ID number into her laptop, which she had connected to the local exchange. A file appeared onscreen with his photograph. Karen clicked on the 'medical files' option and a dialogue box appeared. She clicked on 'blood type and associated records' and hit the print key. She then opened the envelope of photos that the police officer had given her. She held them up against the light of an overhead fluorescent tube. Small sprinklings of blue were visible where the chemical reaction had detected haemoglobin.

Karen checked all the photographs and noted that there appeared to be six individual areas of blood remains. She opened the test tube that Maria Papagalos had prepared for her. She put it inside the PE-6800 blood analysis system and set the parameters to run tests for DNA, blood type, blood group, and blood antigens. Dr Laos knew that the accuracy of the results would depend entirely upon the condition of the blood that had been collected. The solution that Maria Papagalos had placed it in would ensure that any remnants of the blood quality were enhanced.

The blood analysis system started whirring as it split and separated the sample inside the test tube to fit the parameters that Dr Laos had specified. She checked the polymerase chain reaction and variable number tandem repeats that were present in the file on John Riley. She made a note of its unique identifier code and waited whilst the system finalized its analysis of the DNA present. A print-out spewed out the back of the analyzer. Dr Laos noted that there was a degradation rate of 30 per cent from the sample that Papagalos had collected.

The identifier code that the machine had produced seemed to match that from the samples of John Riley's bloodwork. Karen decided that the DNA alone was not enough to confirm the match legally. She waited for the machine to run the further tests she had programmed it for. The next print-out came out of the back of the machine. It detailed blood type.

John Riley's medical file showed that his blood type had been AB. The antigens report from the sample showed an AB match with both type A and B antigens. As Karen expected, no antibodies to either type A or B were present. Based on this fact alone, Karen felt more sure of a match; one that she could confidently confirm. She concluded in her notes that the blood sample found in Little Sam's vehicle was indeed a match to that of John Riley's, meaning that at some point he had been in the vehicle.

More importantly, it also meant that at some point he had suffered an injury consistent with that of a significant level; the pattern of blood stains suggested that, where Riley would not have likely been killed in the vehicle itself, his dead body had more than likely been transported in it.

Thursday August 23, 1.15 a.m.
Makarios Avenue Intersection
Limassol
Cyprus

Inspector Chris Haws had arrived with Danny Mills and his team of six officers in two unmarked vehicles at 1 a.m. He had told Danny to stay dressed as he was to further give the appearance that he had been sleeping rough since he had fled from the base. The officers that would accompany Danny Mills were all dressed casually. Inspector Haws had been sure to pick three of his youngest officers and had told them to say that they were officer cadets, like Danny, if asked by anyone at the club.

The remaining three military policemen were instructed to keep their distance from Danny and his 'friends'. All had been fitted with wires that would allow Inspector Haws to listen in on what was being said. He had the capacity also to communicate back to his team when needed. The hidden earpieces that they wore were so minute that it would require a magnifying glass to be able to see them with the naked eye. The wires that Danny wore were more sophisticated than those that the others had been equipped with.

They had to be, by necessity, far smaller, as he was still wearing a T-shirt. He had asked Inspector Haws whether he should dirty his face a little.

'No,' the inspector had replied. 'You look rough enough already.'

Chris Haws knew that the time to catch Sergii Filatov was now or never; with Charalambos dead, Stanislav Young in custody on a murder charge, and Littleton's body in the mortuary at the base, Filatov formed the last piece of the puzzle to be solved. His counterpart, Inspector Dimitris

Andreou, was of the same opinion.

They had spent time before leaving the base discussing the death of Charalambos. Andreou had told his colleagues in Paphos not to allow Stanislav Young or Rafaela to make any calls until Filatov was caught. He didn't want Filatov to realize that Charalambos was already dead and disappear. Events had, as David Littleton had written in his suicide note, moved quickly over the last few days. Charalambos and Filatov had, as the police had long suspected, allowed their own greed to catch up with them.

It was thanks to Charalambos' public announcement of his involvement with the British bases and the determination of Detective Andreas Ioannou that links had been formed, which now resulted in Inspector Haws and Inspector Andreou and their teams assembling outside Colours Nightclub, in one final drive to rid the local community of the scourge that was Sergii Filatov.

Inspector Andreou found himself in a somewhat different position to that of Chris Haws and his team. He and his team had the authority to carry weapons, which they would use as necessary, as they were officers of the Republic of Cyprus. Andreou had arrived slightly earlier than Inspector Haws as he had taken a team of twenty-one officers with him.

All were kitted with full combat outfits and riot shields. Each officer carried an FMK 9C1 9mm handgun and mace. They had been careful to arrive at the intersection from different angles and streets, to ensure that they drew less attention than necessary. Approaching in nine separate teams from different directions, the officers walked in groups of two.

Andreou had given them their orders. Four teams would be positioned at street level, two officers in each; a further four teams of two would make their way to the rooftops of the four corners of the intersection. The remaining five officers had been instructed to head to the rear of the nightclub and find a concealed position and await further orders. Inspector Haws had agreed with Inspector Andreou that he would wait outside the club with Andreou and listen to the events that would take place inside. Andreou would take the initiative for sending his officers in as required. With all members of the assault team now in place, Inspector Haws addressed Danny Mills directly. He checked his watch. The time was approaching 2 a.m.

'Danny, are you ready?'

'As ready as I'll ever be, sir,' replied Mills.

Haws turned and addressed the three

officers that would pose as Danny Mills' friends.

'Follow Danny's lead; he knows what to say. At the first sign of danger, I want you all out of there.'

The officers confirmed that they understood. He then contacted the other officers that would pose as clubbers.

'I want you to go into the club ten minutes after Danny.'

Danny got out of the concealed vehicle and made his way across the road. He put on a convincing limp and walked straight to the staircase that led into Colours Nightclub. Inspector Andreou approached Chris Haws. He was about to speak but was interrupted by the sound of a voice in his earpiece. He spoke in Greek to one of his officers and turned back to Chris Haws.

'Filatov just parked his vehicle at the back of the club.' He relayed the same message to all of the officers on his team.

Danny Mills stood at the top of the steps. As he looked down, his eyes were met by those of the man at the door. Danny recognized him as Igor.

'What are you doing back here so soon?' Igor asked him, as Mills hobbled down the stairs. 'Sergii didn't want you back until the weekend.'

'I know,' said Danny, 'but I had nowhere else to go.'

'Let the boy in,' roared Sergii Filatov from the top of the staircase.

His sudden appearance behind Danny Mills took Igor by surprise. Danny looked over his shoulder behind him and acted as best as he could.

'Sergii, I'm so pleased to see you,' he said, with a hint of desperation. 'I didn't know where to go. My friend Phil killed himself.'

Sergii ignored him. 'Are these boys with you?' he asked, pointing at the three undercover cops.

'Yes, sir, they are. I've been on the run since Tuesday afternoon when I found Phil. These are my friends. I knew I could trust them to meet me here tonight.'

'Is that so?' asked Filatov, studying the faces of each individually. His large eyes grew small and beady as he appeared to doubt Danny's authenticity.

'If you've been on the run since Tuesday, then how did you manage to contact your friends?' he hissed.

It wasn't a question that Danny Mills had expected. 'I, err, I managed to call one of them from a phone box. I only had a little bit of change in my pocket. I thought it was the best thing to do.' Danny tried not to look scared as he heard his own trembling voice betray the truth. Sergii Filatov again ignored him.

He turned to face Danny squarely. 'Look at the state of you. I can't have one of my employees looking like that. Come inside, Danny, and get yourself a drink.'

'Can I bring my friends too?' Mills asked, aware that he was pushing Filatov and fearful too of Sergii's cold and unemotional expression.

He watched as Sergii simply threw a half-second glance at Danny's friends.

'No, not yet. They can wait here a while,' he replied. He put his arm around Danny's shoulders and pushed him in through the front door.

24

'Why do you look so concerned, Danny?' asked Filatov, his voice loud above the noise from the DJ box.

'It's probably just the stress of the past few days catching up on me,' Danny lied in response. He hadn't heard anything through his earpiece from the outside world. He had hoped that Inspector Haws might have called him to reassure his nerves.

'Tell me, Danny, where have you been hiding since you left the base?'

Danny thought quickly. 'Here and there, keeping on the move, Sergii. It's taken me until now to reach Limassol. I've been hiding in fields and sleeping wherever I could find somewhere sheltered.'

Sergii poured him a large glass of vodka. 'You did the right thing, Danny. It seems like we're a team now.' He laughed as he

312

downed his own drink.

'How do you mean?' Danny asked, quickly adding, 'sir.'

'You're not the only one that's lost someone in the past couple of days. I'm sure you remember Little Sam, the one you had the unfortunate misunderstanding with the other night?'

Danny feigned ignorance. 'Oh, yes, I think so. Was he the guy downstairs?'

Filatov moved his large head closer to Danny.

'Yes,' he snarled. 'He was killed whilst out looking for you.'

'For me? Why was he looking for me?'

Filatov looked disappointed. 'Danny, I told you I would be watching you. Surely you remember Stanislav, the nice guy that let you back into the base the other morning? He told me you had gone missing. Being a concerned kind of guy, I decided to ask Little Sam to look for you. I must say, I'm impressed you came here tonight, though.'

'Why, Sergii?' asked Danny.

Filatov's eyes narrowed as he considered his response. 'It means you trust me more than you do your superiors on the base.' He poured himself another drink. 'That says a lot about a man, Danny. My only question is why you brought those guys outside with you.'

'You told me to, Sergii.'

Filatov contemplated Danny's words. 'In that case, they can come in shortly. Do you think they would be interested in having some of the same stuff that Little Sam gave you the other night?'

Danny knew that he had to get Filatov to admit to having supplied cocaine to him so that the inspector and his men could move in.

'They might be. I didn't tell them, of course, that they would be offered that here.'

'You're a smart kid, Danny.'

'What am I going to do now, Sergii? Now that I'm not welcome back at the base? How am I going to get clothes and make money?'

'I'll set you up with everything you need.'

'But what use am I to you, Sergii, if I can't get the soldiers back at the base to come here?'

Filatov looked into his glass. 'Forget the bases, Danny. I get a feeling there's not much more business to be done there. But there's plenty here.' He waved his arms around the club.

'What can I do here?' asked Danny.

Before Danny had the opportunity to respond, Danny heard Inspector Haws' voice in his concealed earpiece. At first he heard Inspector Haws informing Inspector Andreou that he was doing well. Danny assumed that

314

Chris Haws was talking about him and tried to keep his face still so that Filatov would not see any suspicious signs.

He then heard Inspector Haws talking clearly.

'Danny, it's Inspector Haws. Try not to show that you can hear my voice. Ask Sergii if your friends can join you now.'

'There's lots you can do here, Danny. You may be a skinny fella but some of the best men I've worked with have been your size. You've got your military training. You know how to work a gun, I assume?'

'Of course, Sergii. But what would I need a gun for?'

'You never know, Danny. There's always times they are needed.'

'Can my friends come in now?' Danny asked, hesitantly, feeling a little more confident that he had Sergii's trust. A deeper level of thought told him that trust was not something that Sergii Filatov would ever bestow on another. He quickly pushed the uncomfortable reality of such a scenario out of his mind.

Sergii called a barman over and told him to let the three men waiting outside with Igor into the club. Danny watched as they walked in, a wave of relief rushing through his stressed and anxious mind. He watched as they pulled up some bar-seats a couple of metres away from Danny and Sergii.

Sergii turned back to Danny. 'There's time to introduce me to your friends later. But first, there's something I want to show you downstairs. Let's just say it's the key to your future.'

'Downstairs?' Danny said, aware that he had blurted the word out.

'Yes, Danny. Is there something wrong with that?' asked Filatov.

Outside on the main street Inspector Haws sent a message to the three undercover cops posing as Danny's friends telling them to follow him from a distance. He then spoke again directly to Danny and Danny kept his face as unresponsive as he could.

'It's OK, Danny,' said Inspector Haws. 'Go with Sergii. We're right behind you.'

'No, Sergii, there's nothing wrong with that at all. I just remember the other night, that's all,' Danny explained.

'That was before we were friends,' replied Filatov, escorting Danny to the black curtain that led to the flight of stairs downstairs. 'You've got nothing to worry about this time.'

They walked down the stairs, Danny one step behind Filatov.

'Behind this door, Danny, there's more than you saw the other night,' Filatov

316

explained as he stuck his key in the door and opened it into the room where Danny and Phil had been held by Little Sam.

Danny felt a cold chill move down his spine as he recalled the last time he had been in the room. Two of the people that had been there, Phil Wakely and Little Sam, were now dead. As they walked into the room, Filatov closed the door behind them. Danny felt relieved as he noticed that Sergii hadn't locked the door.

'What am I looking at, Sergii?' he asked.

'You'll see.'

Filatov moved to the far wall and with his hands started to push at certain areas of what looked like a normal concrete partition. The sound of metal rubbing against concrete started as a gentle rumble and grew louder. Filatov stepped back. The wall parted in two halves and a wooden door came into view.

'Wow,' exclaimed Danny, unable to repress his genuine thrill at the spectacle.

Filatov ignored him and pulled another key from his pocket. He pushed it into the lock on the wooden door and clicked it open. As the door swung inwards, Danny could say only, 'Holy shit.'

The secret room concealed a small mountain of what appeared to be cocaine. Despite his astonishment, Danny estimated that there must be at least several thousand small bags of the drug piled up one on top of the other.

'Holy shit indeed, Danny,' said Filatov, turning back to face him. 'Why do you think I'm showing you this?'

Danny answered slowly. He had noticed that the tone in Sergii's voice no longer sounded quite as friendly as it had a few moments previously.

'You said that down here was the key to my future, so I guess it's because this is how I'm going to make my living from now on?'

Filatov laughed at him. 'In a manner of speaking, Danny, yes. Except *you* won't be living. This is where you're going to die. You've been lying to me. Tell me, do you think I'm really that stupid?' he shouted.

'What do you mean? What have I done wrong?' Danny asked, hoping that the inspector was listening to what was going on.

'Your so-called friends. They're not your army buddies. They're fucking cops. Igor recognized them as soon as they came in. Stanislav gave us photos of all of the cops at the base a long time ago.'

Sergii reached into his pocket and pulled out a large serrated knife. He stroked it tenderly. 'This is why I've been so successful in business, Danny,' he continued. 'Whenever people try and pull a fast one on me, I always get the upper hand.' He hissed the words as he spoke.

'Get the hell in there!' screamed Inspector Andreou down his radio.

Three of his officers that were in the car park at the rear of the building sprinted to the steps that led to the entrance, their FMK 9C1 9mm handguns and riot shields in front of them. Igor looked up, expecting company, and pulled out a gun himself. He aimed a shot to the top of the stairs as the first cop came into sight. It hit the riot shield and flew off in the opposite direction. He aimed again as all three cops descended on him. The cop in the middle rushed down the stairs and sprayed Igor's face with mace. He keeled over in pain, aiming his gun again, and tried to fire.

Igor's five-year tenure at the door of Colours Nightclub came to an abrupt end there and then as the cop flanking up the rear aimed a single bullet and hit him directly in the abdomen. The bullet pierced his stomach and ricocheted its way through his gut and out the other side.

Sergii Filatov rushed towards Danny with the sharp knife in his hands as he heard the music stop in the club. One of Inspector Andreou's men had pulled the DJ box from its power source. People upstairs were screaming in confusion as riot police entered the building and ordered them all to the floor. Danny moved to the side of the room, hoping that the door would open and police would any second come to his rescue.

'You little prick!' screamed Filatov as he raced after him.

Danny saw that Sergii was quick on his feet but his movements were lumbered and awkward. His adrenalin kicked in.

'Come on, then, you fat fucker!' he screamed. 'Come and get me if you can.'

Sergii's face turned a dark red as the rage kicked in.

Danny lowered himself to the floor and raced forwards as fast as he could manage. He extended his arms wide as his head went through Filatov's open legs. His arms acted like a barrier, bringing Filatov's legs back on his own body. Filatov fell to the floor, his knife skittering out of his hand across the room. The door swung open and a group of cops piled in. Danny saw Inspector Andreou taking the lead. Filatov, finding his footing, made a crouched move for the serrated knife. Andreou delivered a quick blow with his boot to Filatov's gut, sending him tumbling again. Filatov let out a scream of pain but managed to get a hold of his weapon.

He swung it in the air, aiming at Inspector

Andreou's throat. Danny looked on in shock, and time seemed to slow as another cop moved quickly to help his boss. He used his baton to strike the knife from Filatov's hands. The blow sent it spinning up into the air, its thick grip-handle hitting the ceiling above.

The blade dropped straight back down at high speed and embedded itself into Filatov's leg, severing the femoral artery. He let out a high-pitched wail and collapsed as a fountain of blood jetted from the knife-wound. Danny watched as the dying man dragged himself along the concrete floor towards the hidden room containing the stash of cocaine bags. As his body went limp, Sergii Filatov let out one last gurgled breath.

25

Saturday August 25, 10.30 a.m.
Central Command
Episkopi Garrison
Western Sovereign Base Area
Cyprus

'Dr Laos, are you sure there isn't any way we can convince you stay a little longer?'

The major general walked around the front of his desk and spoke to Karen. He had asked that the office he had been temporarily assigned would certainly not be the same one that Littleton had killed himself in. Despite the fact that the room had been thoroughly cleaned, the major general's wishes were respected. A large padlock had been inserted into the door, closing it for the foreseeable future.

'I appreciate the sentiment, Mr Morrison,' answered Karen, 'but there is really no more work for me to do here. Littleton's dead, as are both Filatov and Charalambos. Inspector Haws tells me that Stanislav Young is facing a life sentence for murder and we've managed to eradicate the drugs problem here.'

She thought about the events that had occurred over the past week and how, only five days ago, she had been back at her apartment in Salford Quays, before her trip had even started.

'I understand, Dr Laos,' the major general replied, sounding genuinely saddened to see Karen leave. 'However, whilst it may be true that the case you came to help us with has been solved, you still haven't had the chance to leave the base and explore the island.'

Karen thought about the major general's words. It was certainly true that she had spent her entire time at the base. She had more than fulfilled her scheduled work hours; the previous day having been taken up with completing Littleton's autopsy and taking blood samples from the personnel that had tested positive for illicit substances during the urine-testing agenda.

Dr Laos found that her prediction had been pretty much correct. In all, 358 personnel had tested positive; 340 for cocaine and the remaining number for both cocaine and cannabis. Major General Morrison had decided to respect Littleton's wish that the staff be offered treatment rather than being punished. There were, after all, many victims left in the wake of Filatov and Charalambos' deaths.

The major general found himself wishing that Andrew had been afforded the same opportunity that he would now extend to the personnel that had tested positive for drug misuse.

'You're right, Mr Morrison,' Karen said. 'If it's OK with you, I think I will stay around for a few more days.'

'Excellent,' replied the major general. 'I'll cancel your flight out this evening and rebook you to depart on Wednesday next week. That should give you some time to relax.'

Karen thought about the promise she had made to Inspector Andreou. She would contact him and ask him to help her track the origins of her family name and to give her a tour of the island. She turned to Morrison.

'And how about you? How long do you think you'll stay here?'

The major general checked his diary. 'As long as necessary, Dr Laos. At my stage in life, I'm incredibly lucky to have a chance like this. My wife is slowly healing from the loss of Andrew under such awful circumstances. I think she finds being here better than going back to a life of retirement. We've decided to bury Andrew here on the island. He loved Cyprus and we all have fond memories of his childhood here.'

Karen leaned in closer. 'It will take time,

Mr Morrison. But from what I see, you're doing an excellent job at honouring Andrew's memory.'

He smiled his appreciation. 'To be honest, Dr Laos, my wife and I have been talking about permanently relocating back to Cyprus. It seems fitting somehow, even after my temporary tenure as the commanding officer here comes to an end.'

'In that case,' Karen replied, 'the future looks a lot more positive than it did a few days ago.'

The major general walked to the door to his office and opened it wide. 'Dr Laos, you're officially on vacation. Go and enjoy yourself, and make sure you stop by before you leave next week.'

Karen collected her bag. 'I will do,' she assured him as she walked out into the corridor and headed outside, her head full of thoughts about the Laos family that she was planning to track down with the help of Dimitris Andreou.

Other titles published by Ulverscroft:

PEROXIDE HOMICIDE

Matthew Malekos

When working a night shift at Manchester's inner-city morgue, forensic pathologist Karen Laos finds herself with the body of an unknown male, apparently murdered by a killer she had pursued six years before. Karen reunites with ageing policeman Detective Inspector James Roberts and together they must identify, locate and catch the killer taunting them both. With an appetite for ritualistic murder and an array of alarming and unusual methods, there is a real threat that this killer will elude their grasp and strike again, leaving only mutilated victims in his wake . . .

RANDOM TARGETS

James Raven

A sniper launches a series of deadly attacks on Britain's motorways, striking during rush hour and causing total carnage. No one knows who he is, or why he's doing it — and as the death toll rises, fear grips the nation. It's up to DCI Jeff Temple of the Major Investigations department to bring the killing spree to an end — but, as he closes in on the sniper, Temple makes a shocking discovery about the motive behind the attacks. A ghastly precedent has been set, and Temple realizes that any motorway driver risks becoming a random target . . .